THE RAVEN

BearManor Media
P.O. Box 1129
Duncan, OK 73534-1129

Phone: 580-252-3547
Fax: 814-690-1559

www.bearmanormedia.com

The Raven by Eunice Sudak was
First published as a Lancer Book - 1963
First BearManor Media Edition 2012
The Raven was produced and released
By American International, 1963
Edited and book designed by Philip J. Riley ©2012
"The Making of *The Raven*" ©*Lawrence French, 2012*
All photographs from the Lawrence French Collextion

The Nightmares Series is being published to preserve original movie tie-in novels that were printed many years ago, on the old style pulp paper. It will also include several very rare movie tie-in titles in the horror film genre. We hope these reprints will allow them to last into the new century.

Philip J. Riley's
NIGHTMARE SERIES

Brides of Dracula
The Revenge of Frankenstein

THE RAVEN

By
Eunice Sudak

Based on an original screenplay
by Richard Matheson

Philip J Riley's

NIGHTMARE SERIES

BearManor Media

"To Danielle Zuk and Ken Cocuzzo: Two Shining Lights in a otherwise very Dark Tunnel !!!!!"

Quote The Raven.... " Evermore..."
THE RAVEN
By Richard A. Ekstedt

"The Raven"......... Karloff! Price!! Lorre!!! Court!!!!!! Nicholson!!!!!!!!!!!! ROGER CORMAN!!

What can you possibly say about the sight of ole Smilin' Jack (Nicholson), wearing that Robin Hood type outfit (complete with feather in his hat), talking in his New Jersey accent, trying to pass himself off as Peter Lorre's son?...GAAWWWD!!!.... I mean, outside of "The Terror", where he is wearing the uniform of a French Army Officer in Napoleon's Army and speaking English with a New Jersey accent, it really doesn't get any better than this when it comes to a ... (LOUD TRUMPETTTTT!!!!!!!) ......ROGER (Flowers coming down from the sky!!!) .... CORMAN... (Vast, Growing, Ever LOUDER Cheering Crowd!!!!) ....FILM........ (Sounds Of Cheering and Marching Band Music!!!)!!!!!!!!!

To HELL(!!!!!) with the over opinionated "Expert" Art Fart, Intellectual/snob, wine and cheese, pinky in the air while taking tea, and "braying" Ingmar Bergman, Federico Fellini or Woody Allen crowd!!!!

This, people, is MY (MY!.... DO YOU HEAR ME??.... MY!!!!) idea of a great movie!!!!!!!!!!!!!!!!!!

"The Raven", not to be confused with the 1935 Universal film of the same name (that starred Boris Karloff and Bela Lugosi), deals the comedic tone (mis)adventures of a group of preposterous practitioners of permutation, particularly partial sorcerer Dr. Erasmus Craven (Vincent Price).

Dr Craven is mourning the death of his second wife, the beautiful buxom (or top-heavy) Lenore (Hazel Court), for the last several years to the concern of his daughter (from his first wife), Estelle (Olive Sturgess). That night, The Raven (with the voice of Peter Lorre) arrives to beg Craven to return him to his original human form. After brewing a potion for the bewildered bird, it takes effect and The Raven is transformed into budding wizard, Dr. Bedlo (Lorre). Dr. Bedlo tells Craven he has seen Lenore's spirit , a prisoner at the castle of the famed dark wizard Dr. Scarabus (Boris Karloff). Craven, Bedlow, Estelle and Bedlo's son, Rexford (the ever deranged Jack Nicholson) decide to investigate Bedlo's tale. At the castle the story then turns to deceit unveiled and magic unleashed to a comic conclusion. When Roger Corman decided to film "The Raven", he decided to approach it in a different direction. He felt that all the Poe movies up to that point were getting too similar in tone (somber) and writer Richard Matheson, who did the screenplays of most of the Poe films, suggested a comedy was the way to go (and since it was originally a poem about a depressed man talking to a bird, not really making much of a plot in itself, it was used as a springboard for an original tale) . Roger Corman thought it was a great idea and the result was the entire cast having a great time making it, with one very small exception-The Raven! The trained bird insisted on crapping on everyone and star Jack Nicholson was reported to have said, "I hate that bird!"

Vincent Price was once again in the lead, getting to remove himself from the gloomy performances of a tortured soul and instead, does his hand at comedy with a delightful array of facial expressions (His role in "His Kind Of Woman", with stars Robert Mitchum and Jane Russell, show his ability at comedy, playing an ego charged actor, sure brings this to my mind!). Boris Karloff, brought on board, was able to pull off his delicious role as the evil Doctor Scarabus- a comedic version of Liam McGinnis's Karswell from "Night (Curse) Of The Demon", which (witch?) is a delight, as he tries to win the cold bitchy heart (and "Charms") of British actress Hazel Court, (who had a starring role in the non-Vincent Price Poe film, "The Premature Burial", which starred Ray Milland , along with Heather Angel, who was best remembered for her starring role in the classic werewolf thriller, "The Undying Monster", in 1942) known well for her roles in Hammer Films, "The Curse Of Frankenstein" and "The Man Who Could Cheat Death". Canadian Olive Sturgess, who had appeared in "The Kettles In The Ozarks" (and would later appear also in "Requiem For A Gunfighter"), got to show her talent as the perky Estelle Cravan. She is also best remembered for "The Bob Cummings Show" on television.

But it is Peter Lorre who delighted filmgoers by stealing the show as the foul tempered, sniveling, spiteful, incompetent wizard, Dr. Adolphus Bedlo. Peter had worked with Vincent Price in "The Black Cat" segment when Roger Corman filmed the trilogy, "Poe's Tales Of Terror", in 1962, and Lorre would be reunited with Vincent Price and Boris Karloff (as well as Joyce Jamison from "Black Cat" along with veteran actor Basil Rathbone) for "The Comedy Of Terrors" in 1964, directed by Jacques Tourneur.

Roger Corman, on the "Raven" dvd, recounts how Peter Lorre would improvise and adlib his lines, which sometime would throw off Boris Karloff (who was classical old school style), and in turn, Vincent Price would take on the job of being the mediator between the two. Peter Lorre's Doctor Bedlow also has a hilarious relationship with his screen son, Rexford Bedlow , played with dim light bulb perfection by Jack Nicholson, as a son trying to win his father's love (and of course the joke is that Bedlow CAN'T STAND THE SIGHT of his handsome, lean, idolizing boy!) It really comes off great with Peter Lorre, who improvised especially for these scenes, getting into his role, smacking and calling Nicholson various names in the movie!.

Roger Corman came up with an idea of using a crane in the climax of the film, working with Floyd Crosby, where Vincent Price and Boris Karloff, have the delightful "Wizard's Duel". It was filmed in a way where Vincent Price, shit-eating grin on his face, ends up floating up into the air to Les Baxter's rendition of circus themes. This was wonderfully pulled off and still, to this day, cannot help to make the viewer share Price's grin!

Daniel Haller, who was the art director, reused sets from previous Poe films as well as using surviving sets from classic past films of Hollywood productions (to stretch the $200,000 budget). And like past Poe productions he shot, it gave Director of Photography,

Floyd Crosby , to take the advantage of this to capture a specific look for the film.

"The Raven" was released on January 25, 1963 to great response to both critics and the general public. The film earned a reputed $1,499,275 and after p/s tv and vhs prints, a new widescreen life, first on laserdisc and now on dvd (with digital overhaul) to a new generation of fans.

When "The Raven' wrapped up filming, Roger Corman still had three days left on his agreement with Boris Karloff and quickly wrote a new story, using the standing sets, to feature Karloff and Nicholson, calling it "The Terror"! Beside Roger Corman, also working on this film, included Jack Hill and Frances Ford Coppola, which resulted in a drive-in delight that holds up to this day!!!!

The book you now hold in your hand is a film tie-in edition of the original Lancer paperback that was printed in 1963 by Eunice Sudak, based upon Richard Matheson's screenplay.

This book, and others in "The Nightmare Series", belong to a rapidly fading to extinction series of film books, that were never reprinted for the most part and would have vanished from memory (and many of these books that survive command high prices from dealers of rare or obscure tomes!). Philip J. Riley, in the process of brushing strange black feathers out of his hair, while muttering about the taste of some brew he tasted, should (and along with his publisher, Ben Ohmart) be praised beyond measure for restoring these wonderful books back to us to read and compare to the finished film.   For myself, while rubbing my head after Phil conked me with a mace, I am going to sit back before the fire with a sniffer of brandy (plus two aspirin with a grog chaser), with a Mr. Sardonicus smile, and open up this boo....WAIT!!!!!!!........is that a rapping I hear knocking on my chamber's door????????

Richard A. Ekstedt
Somewhere on a misty mountaintop in PA!!!

England at the end of the Middle ages—a time of fear and super-stition, a time when Magic was not just a word but an absolute reality, a time when strange things went Bump in the Night.

Chapter 1

THIS PARTICULAR night was grayed and eerie, foreboding, glum as only early December can be glum. The wind howled. There was no moon. The air was stiff with moisture waiting to become snow.

Dr. Erasmus Craven could feel the dampness nagging at the hollows under his knees. He sighed. Although the stone floor of his study was thick with rugs, although heavy tapestries layered the walls, and the windows, tall ones that looked out over the cliffs, were closed and latched, then blocked by oak shutters, and over these, double-woven silk curtains, it didn't matter. The damp came through. And with the damp, the sense of something ominous, lurking in the night.

A larger fire might have helped, but Dr. Craven didn't call for one. He might have moved closer to what was left of the blaze that had been laid after supper, but he didn't. The room was tangled with deep shadows, and that end in which Dr. Craven sat was almost completely dark. Dr. Craven liked it so.

For a moment his hands rested motionless on the black velvet cloth that covered the top of his desk. He sighed again, and a pale light glimmered about the tips of his fingers. They were smooth, these fingertips, gently rounded and flushed with pink—more like those of a young boy than those of a man in his fifties. The light faded. The, very slowly, the index finger of Dr. Craven's right hand lifted and moved in the air from left to right, leaving, as its wake, a streak of delicately glowing color, which remained, hovering in the air from left to right. And now the second finger moved, and the third, and with each movement one more stroke of shimmering color was created.

Line crossed line, stroke flowed into stroke, as little by little, the movements grew stronger and more definite. Dr. Craven's handsome face was grave. His eyes were tense, eager. A pyramid had been formed. He stared at it with an absorption that was childlike and faintly ludicrous, the absorption of a man who knows he is squandering his gifts, and who, perversely, is pleased by this. Then, raising his left hand, working swiftly, skillfully with it and with his right, he began to embellish, to add squares, cubes, more triangles, a perfectly drawn hexagon, to build in the air above the dark cloth a series of extraordinary geometric design, ridiculously elaborate and fascinatingly complex.

The structure was complete—wonderful and absurd. Dr. Craven smiled to it. But, he thought—but—And without thinking further he began meticulously to fill in the blank spaces. Red for this space. Orange here. And next to it, a vivid blue. Beside the blue—a mossy green perhaps? He was considering this, weighing it, choosing the precise shade and the precise intensity that his green might have, when suddenly, the hall door opened.

Dr. Craven started with surprise.

And deprived of his attention, the entire color pattern disappeared with the sound and the rapidity of a pricked soap bubble.

Dr. Craven's response was a quick gasp, almost a whimper, of infantile dismay. Then assuming an expression of piqued disapproval, he turned toward the door, which was now thrown wide.

"I've brought you your goblet of warm milk, Father." Estelle Craven spoke softly and a trifle tentatively. She knew she had interrupted her father in the midst of his favorite activity, yet, because she felt that activity to be, at best, inconsequential, she could do no more than feign a weak remorse.

Her father understood. Indeed, nodding to her as she approached the desk, he sympathized. She was such a beautiful child— so slight, so fair. Nineteen years old; ready to be a woman.

She set before him the small silver tray she was carrying, then circled the desk to stand at his side.

"Thank you, Estelle," he said, trying now to control his annoyance and to keep the sound of it from his voice.

"It *was* a pretty design, Father." Estelle smiled, and ruffling the shock of his still black hair, bent to kiss him on the forehead.

"Wasn't it?" he answered sadly. Then, looking up at her, he, too, smiled. In this instant she was the parent; he the child, and in need of comfort.

She gazed at him with affection, waited until he had taken the goblet of milk from the tray, raised it to his lips and swallowed a sip. Then, nodding—clearly, she loved him very much—she squeezed his shoulder and said, "I'll leave you to your studies now."

"Yes," Dr. Craven murmured, following her with his eyes as she moved toward the door, went out into the hallway, then shut the door behind her.

Once again the study was shadowed and dark. Dr. Craven sat holding the goblet of milk and smiling quietly at the closed door, which had disappeared from his view. Then, as if compelled, he turned and looked across the room, toward the fireplace, and beside it, the set of open double doors that connected the study with the chapel. His face collapsed into mournfulness. And putting down the milk, spilling a little over the burnished edge of the tray, he stood. Mechanical steps, slow and trancelike, drew him to the chapel doors, where he paused for a moment.

At the distant end of the chapel was the altar, a kind of shrine. A pair of wax tapers guttered in tall wrought-silver holders on either side of the heavy purple cloth with which it was draped. Hanging between them was a large oil portrait in an ovaled mahogany frame.

Erasmus Craven lifted his eyes to the painting , to the beautiful face, all but invisible in the failing light. Yet the face, the woman, was visible to him—as visible and as live and as new as his grief. Walking more slowly even than before, he approached her, stopped when he was halfway across the room, continued, stopped again when he had reached the altar. He leaned against it for an instant. Then, after he had stifled what threatened to become a fit of hopeless sobs, he took two fresh candles from a golden box, lighted them, and used them to replace the others, which he let tumble to the bare stone floor.

The brass plate at the portrait's base could now be read. He mouthed the name that appeared on it—*Lenore Craven*. And the date—*1380-1416*. Then, staring up at the woman who had been his wife, he spoke aloud.

"Come back to me, Lenore." His voice was pleading, pained. "Come back—"

Abruptly, he broke off, freezing to listen to the faint rustle of a skirt as it moved through the doors behind him. The sound was louder now, closer. A hand came down upon his shoulder, and he turn, gasping.

The hand fell away. "I just came back to—" Estelle gestured awkwardly. "I wanted to tell you not to stay up too late."

"I won't my dear," he promised, flat voiced and more than naturally composed, withholding his emotions even as he curbed the impulse to be sharp.

Estelle started to smile, but when she saw that he was about to turn back to the portrait, her lips trembled and refused her. Without meaning to, she frowned instead. He turned, and her gaze followed his.

Now, for several moments, father and daughter stared together at the image of Lenore. At the lustrous ebony hair, elaborately massed above a smooth and exquisitely white expanse of brow; at the gently aristocratic nose; at the wide and teasing lips, parted slightly over a row of small but perfect teeth. And at the eyes, Enormous eyes, impossible to fathom.

"She *has* been dead for over two years now, Father." Estelle spoke reluctantly.

And Erasmus Craven paused before replying. At last, smiling sadly, he said, "You are young, Estelle. The young do not understand grief. To you"—looking at Lenore, he shrugged away his daughter's protest—"to you, she was only a stepmother. To me—she was life."

"I'm sorry, Father." Estelle kissed his cheek, then tip-toed from the room.

Erasmus Craven continued his somber vigil.

It was nearly midnight when, closing the chapel doors after him, he returned to the study and to his desk. Settled into his chair, he was enough at ease to yawn once or twice, but he was still far from the possibility of sleep. Estelle had lighted a candelabrum for him, and thoughtfully, had set it on the small stand to his left. With a defeated little grin of acknowledgment for this, he picked up the goblet of milk and took a sip. The milk had grown cold; worse, it had acquired a faintly musty taste. He put it to one side, yawned, then reached across the desk and pulled over an ancient leather-bound volume. The title on its spine, *Curious Rytes of Magickal Lore,* was barely legible, its gold lettering all but erased by time. He opened the book to the place marked and scanned it for a few moments. Then, shifting slightly in his chair, he began to read.

Some half a dozen books were now open before Dr. Craven. And he was just starting to get interested. Groping at the shelves behind him, he found still another volume and after checking to see that it was the one he wanted, he brought it, too, to the desk. He bent over it, turning page after page until he came to a certain peculiar drawing; then, turning several pages back, he devoted himself to the text.

A series of quick tapping sounds, repeated, then repeated again, failed to disturb him, failed even to make him glance away from his page. "Come in," he said casually, directing his voice toward the hallway door.

Silence.

Then, for the fourth time, the tapping sounds. They were a little louder now, and a little more imperative.

And now Dr. Craven looked up. "*Enter,*" he said.

In answer, there was more tapping. And more.

Exhaling, Dr. Craven cast his eyes heavenward. The tapping stopped. Then it resumed. For a moment, Dr. Craven waited, pressing his hands against the edge of the desk as he glared around the room, saw nothing out of the ordinary. The tapping continued, unceasing now, urgent, angry. And waiting no longer, Dr. Craven strode to the door and opened it.

The hallway was empty of a living soul. Nothing moved in it; nothing so much as stirred. Dr. Craven paced its length, peered into its every shadow—and found nothing, nothing at all.

When he came back to the study he was muttering to himself. He slammed the door shut and started toward his desk. No sooner had the reverberations of the offended door left his ears than he heard the tapping again. He twisted about, startled at first, then uncomfortable, strangely anxious.

The tapping went on.

Dr. Craven made a confused sound, struggled to regain a measure of calm, and at last, when he was able to quiet himself, managed to locate the source of the tapping. It was behind him. It was at one of the windows. He turned.

Not certain whether to be irritated, fascinated, or frightened, he was, in consequence, a little of each. Yet the tapping, grown increasingly vehement, would not allow him to hesitate. Uneasily, he moved to the windows and stood before their silken purple drapes. No hesitation, he reminded himself.

Jerking back the drapes, he reached to open one of the upper shutters. Then he stopped. The tapping was below, near the sill. He lunged at the bottom shutter and pulled it wide. For an instant he was without any sense of balance, stumbling, about to fall. A moment later he was squatting in front of the window, holding the inside sill, and straining to see out. And an instant—less than an instant—later than that, he gasped in horror; then, gripping the sill, he giggled slightly; then he spoke. "Upon my soul—" he said, and lapsed into silence.

Two eyes, black and smooth and gleaming with fury, were fixed upon him. At first he had seen only these. Then he had realized that they were very small eyes, very small indeed—the eyes of a bird, a raven, perched on the outer sill.

Dr. Craven smiled wanly.

The tapping had ceased, and the bird seemed to be wholly occupied with gazing upon him through the pane.

"You want to come in?" Dr. Craven asked.

It pecked wildly at the window.

"Well—" Dr. Craven paused uncertainly. "Well—so you do!"

The bird was quiet now. Its head was tilted as if in contempt. Its eyes followed Dr. Craven, who had moved over to the other side of the window in order to release the catch.

Finally, the window was open.

Dr. Craven shrank away as his visitor stepped promptly and proudly from the outer to the inner sill and then, with a swift flutter of wings, flew across the study and settled itself, shivering, on top of the marble bust of Pallas Athena that had been long ago banished to a dusty shelf over the hallway door.

The bird seemed to be whimpering, making noises that were almost human.

"Upon my soul—" its host observed blankly. After a moment, he closed the window, the shutters, the curtains. "Upon mu soul—" He walked to the door and looked up.

The raven, still shivering was staring down.

"Cold, are you?" Dr. Craven asked, vaguely amused at the spectacle.

"I'd be a lot warmer if you'd get me some wine!"

CHAPTER 2

STUNNED, BLINKING, Dr. Craven sought the support of the wall. He cowered, yet he was unable to take his eyes from the black bird. The bird—the thing—had spoken. It had talked back to him— answered his inane question. From out of that curved and shiny beak had come words—a voice— And wasn't there something familiar—?

"Well?" the bird said, admonishing its dilatory host.

Dr. Craven could respond with no more than a dazed grunt.

The bird flapped its wings, spoke louder. "Don't just stand there *gaping* at me!" It seemed to be losing its temper.

"That voice—" Dr. Craven muttered weakly.

"Will you kindly get me some wine!"

"*Yes!*" Dr. Craven twitched to momentary attention.

"Yes," he repeated, raising a hand to his head, then turning and moving slowly toward that cabinet in which the wines were kept.

With the raven watching, he removed the first decanter, the first glass that came to his trembling fingers, carried them to the desk, opened the decanter, started to pour. "Surely," he told himself, not quite believing it, "surely, this must be a dream."

After a moment's pause, he picked up the filled glass and went to the door, where he stood uncertainly, raising the glass above his head in order to extend it to his guest.

"What do you expect me to do?" the bird asked crossly. "*Hold* it?"

Dr. Craven's mouth fell open, but no sound came out. He lowered the glass, looked at it, then stared at the bird in dismay.

"Oh, never mind," it said, and flew downward, landing on Dr. Craven's left shoulder.

Dr. Craven gasped and went rigid.

The bird remained on his shoulder—waiting. *"Well—?"* it asked.

Gasping again, then swallowing hard, Dr. Craven lifted the glass and held it so that the bird could drink from it.

"Better," the visitor said, almost directly into the ear of its host. Then it bent its head and dipped its ebony beak into the glass, threw back its head and gurgled down the wine. Twice it repeated this process, and then the wine was gone. The bird sighed. "That's more like it."

Dr. Craven stared askance at the bird, which continued to perch on his shoulder. "Upon my soul," he said faintly.

"Never mind your soul," the bird snarled. "Start concentrating on getting me back to my rightful form."

"Rightful—*form?*"

"You don't think I was *born* like this, do you? The bird's tone was heavy with contempt.

"You're under an enchantment," Dr. Craven said, dazed.

"Now you've got it," said his visitor, and thereupon departed his shoulder to fly a sarcastic loop about the room. Then, coming to light on the edge of the desk, it glared at its dumbfounded host and announced in peremptory fashion,

"All right. I'm ready. Let's get to work."

Dr. Craven could say nothing. He could think of nothing to say. He nodded his head without comprehension.

"Well," the raven said, you can begin now." It waited a moment glaring. Then it shouted *Do* something!"

"Do what?" Dr. Craven asked dully.

The bird flapped its wings in agitation, in fury. *"Restore me to my rightful form!"*

Dr. Craven shrank back. "I don't know how, he said, beginning to tremble again.

"Oh, *no."* The bird seemed stunned. It fluffed its glossy black feathers, apparently as a way to help itself think. Then, getting pan-

19

icky, hopping about on top of the desk, it said, "Quickly! Have you got some dried bat's blood in the house?"

The wineglass was still in Dr. Craven's hands. He stared down at it, not sure he had heard correctly. After a moment he opened his fingers, and the glass tumbled silently to the rug. Looking up at the bird, Dr. Craven said, "I beg your—"

He was not allowed to finish the question. "Bat's blood!" the raven shouted. "Dried bat's blood!"

"*No.*" Dr. Craven grimaced in disgust.

"How about chain links from a gallows bird?" the raven asked.

Dr. Craven shook his head.

"Jellied spiders?"

Another shake of the head. Another no.

"Rabbit's lard?" The raven's tones became increasingly shrill. "Hartshorn spirits? Dead man's hair?"

Dr. Craven's head was shaking a little faster than he meant it to. He put up a hand to control it. Sickened, he said, I don't keep such things in the house."

"And you call yourself a *magician?*" The raven groaned. "This is too much."

"One moment," Dr. Craven said, suddenly remembering.

"*Yes?*" The bird came back to the edge of the desk and assumed a position of urgent attention.

"It's just possible that there might be some of those"— Dr. Craven frowned as he tried to think of the proper term—"those *ingredients* in my father's old laboratory."

"Don't you *know?*" the bird asked, impatient, unbelieving.

"No," Dr. Craven said. He was somewhat calmer now. "I haven't been down there since he died—more than twenty years ago."

"Well, let's go and see," the bird insisted. "I don't care to remain like this the rest of my life."

"You mean those"—Dr. Craven stopped to frown again, then to gaze for a moment at his visitor— "those *things* you requested are going to change you back to what you were?" He took a step forward, toward the desk—then another step—moving slowly, peering at the bird. The voice, he thought, something in the inflections—? He knew he had heard it before. If he could just catch it, place it—

"Come on," the raven interrupted, and taking sudden flight, landed on the shoulder of its startled host. "Let's *go!*"

Dr. Craven jerked to a halt. His eyes rolled sideways to regard the bird, which he saw as a huge black blur. He could feel the sleekness of black feathers against his cheek, a kind of oily quality, a frightening prickliness about the edges. That voice, he thought once more, if he could just—

"Let's *go!*" the bird repeated, giving Dr. Craven a sharp slap with its closer wing. *"Now!"*

Dr. Craven's hand started up and out. He meant to rub the offended side of his face. Then, realizing that it would be impossible to do this without touching the bird, he quickly let the hand fall. He inhaled hard, let the breath hiss out of his lungs, and bearing the raven with him, went to get the candelabrum from the small metal stand beside the desk.

It was unnecessary for the bird to encourage him further, either by insults or by slaps. He picked up the candelabrum—with his left hand, for it was on his right shoulder that the bird was riding. Then, setting his teeth edge to edge, he turned about and proceeded ;at a brisk pace across the study and into the shadowy hallway, through it, and thence through a maze of dark and narrow passages to the door that opened on the cellar staircase.

No word was spoken. But the cellar door creaked and groaned on its rusted iron hinges, and Dr. Craven's hurried footsteps resounded on the stone stairs, then on the stone of a wide corridor, and a narrower one, dank and bloomy, that connected with it. At the start of a range of low arches, he paused and glanced timorously at the raven; then, stooping a little in deference to his passenger, and slowing his steps to avoid slipping on the damp stone floor, he moved on until, moments later, he was in front of the laboratory.

"How strange to be down here after all these years," he said, gazing apprehensively at the locked door, at the scabrous layers of dirt with which it was encrusted, the huge cobwebs that hung in its corners.

The bird, not interested in such things, responded with an impatient grunt.

Whereupon, Dr. Craven, grimacing uncertainly, put his hand

into the small niche beside the door, groped for an instant, then unhooked and pulled out the key. It, and his hand too, came away damp and covered with broken cobwebs. He wiped both against the wall, dropping the corroded iron key when he heard it screech shrilly and hideously on the stones; retrieving it from the floor, where it had clattered into a watery crevice near his feet; and then, with some difficulty, managing to insert it in the disused lock. It turned more quickly than might have been expected.

But the door itself was stuck. Dr. Craven pushed at it. It refused to open. He pushed harder. Still it refused. At last he brought up his foot and fetched the door an angry kick just below the base of the lock. The door shuddered slightly and began to grate ajar; after which Dr. Craven, pushing strenuously, was able to open it far enough so that he and his guest could enter the laboratory.

When he was just inside, he stopped. He was coughing, choking on the pale cloud of dust that the opening door had stirred into motion. The raven had temporarily taken flight. After a moment it returned, grunting, to his shoulder. The dust had settled. Dr. Craven's eyes burned, as did his throat, but the coughing spasm was over. He held up the candelabrum and looked around uneasily.

The laboratory was a spectral place—low ceilinged, airless, acrid with memory—a place of sorceries and invocations. In its center was a great worktable littered with apparatus—bowls and breakers, mortars, pestles, copper tubing menacingly twisted, copper retorts streaked and blackened by time. Two benches stood at either side of the table. Shelves lined the walls. On them were books in disarray, odd-shaped jars, bottles, boxes, urns, and strange parchments, many of them partially enrolled to reveal mysterious symbols, evil designs. A skeleton hung suspended from a beam. Twin skulls on matching pedestals flanked the door. And everywhere, there was dust; everywhere, there were cobwebs, puddles of stagnant moisture, patches of cheese-like mold, and of rot.

Dr. Craven closed his eyes for a moment. When he opened them he addressed himself to the bird. "What is it you need again?"

"Dried bat's blood," the raven answered condescendingly, "chain links from a gallows bird, rabbit's—"

"Slowly," Dr. Craven interrupted. "Slowly. One thing at a time, please." He moved to the shelves against the far wall and reached for a jar. Then, abruptly, he jerked back his hand, blew on it, shook it hard before him. And an enormous spider, dung colored, hairy legged, fat, dropped to the floor and scrabbled off into the shadows. Swallowing, Dr. Craven watched it, looking faint and slightly bilious as he tried to overcome his revulsion.

"*Now* what is it?" the raven asked, falsely patient.

"Nothing." Dr. Craven's voice was weak and totally devoid of conviction. He swallowed again; then gingerly, he picked up the jar, and after rubbing his thumb over the dusty label, read what was inside. Again, he looked as if he were going to be sick.

"What's that?" The bird leaned forward on his shoulder.

"Entrails of—troubled horse."

"No, no" the bird said irritably. "Put it back."

Dr. Craven did as he was told. Then, picking up a box, he blew the dust from its top, coughed, and tried to read the faded handwriting on the label.

"What's *that?*" The bird had hopped over to one of the side shelves and was perching there, glaring at his host.

Dr. Craven brought the candelabrum a little closer to the box, peered a little harder at the label. But couldn't make it out. He glanced up at the raven. "I—can't read it."

"Well," the bird said crossly, "Look *inside* then."

Sighing, Dr. Craven set the candelabrum on the floor.

Then, very slowly, he opened the lid of the box, and very quickly, he slammed it shut. He was not quite ready to believe what he had seen. Accordingly, he opened the box again, even more slowly this time. Then he gasped and turned pale. The box was filled with eyeballs, some gleaming, some shriveled, staring up at him from out of their own foul ooze.

"What is it?" the raven demanded.

Dr. Craven had closed the box and was sliding it gently back onto the shelf. "I'd"—he gave it a final push—"I'd rather not discuss it if you don't mind."

The bird sniffed contemptuously.

And Dr. Craven, gritting his teeth and pulling himself up to his full stature, forthwith proceeded to explore another shelf, looking at the labels on the various containers and summarily rejecting each in its turn, until at last, he came upon one that seemed right. He faced the raven. "You did say—dead man's hair, didn't you?"

"Yes. That's one of the prime ingredients."

Nodding sadly, Dr. Craven picked up the box and carried it to the worktable. Then he returned to the shelves and to his searching on them.

A short while later there were some ten jars, bottles, and boxes sitting together on the worktable's top. Dr. Craven, his face tight with distaste, was stirring the contents of a small copper caldron, which he had suspended from a hook-like device over an arrangement of burning candles. The raven was now perched on one of the skulls beside the door. Dr. Craven glanced inquiringly at it.

"Now the tongue of a vulture," the raven said, instructing him.

Obedient—but reluctantly so—Dr. Craven found a pair of tweezers, which he used to pick one of the withered black tongues from the open box in which it reposed. Holding the tongue well away from himself, he took it to the caldron and dropped it in. It splashed. And the bubbling stew hissed and whistled and seemed almost to be screaming a complaint—or perhaps an oath—while, seemingly from the very bottom of the caldron, a particularly noxious yellow vapor rose, curled over the caldron's edge, and slowly extended itself toward Dr. Craven's nostrils. With a pained grimace, he stepped back, averting his face.

"But the raven could allow none of this. "Come *on*," it snarled at him. "Come *on*."

"Yes," he said weakly and began again to stir his stew trying the while to stand as far removed from it as possible.

The raven watched in silence from atop the skull on which it was still perched.

Approximately ten minutes elapsed, Dr. Craven stirring steadily but somewhat less than enthusiastically. The vapor was gone. The contents of the caldron had thickened almost into gumminess and had turned a vile greenish-black. The aroma—the stench—was, if anything, worse. Dr. Craven turned to the bird. "Is that all of it? he asked hopefully.

"You've got the jellied spiders in there?"

Pressing his lips together, Dr. Craven nodded.

"The eye of a white weasel?"

He nodded again.

"You didn't forget the dead man's hair?"

He shook his head. "No," he murmured.

"That should do it then," the raven said. "Hand it over."

Dr. Craven was aghast. "You mean to *consume* It?" He stared at the bird.

"What did you *think* I was going to do?" the raven asked. "*Bathe* in it?"

Withdrawing from the caldron the heavy iron rod with which he had been stirring, Dr. Craven used it now in a gesture of defeat. He shrugged. Then, setting aside the rod, he found two thick cloth pads, put one in each hand, and lifted the hot caldron away from the flames. He reeled slightly—the smell of his concoction was all but overpowering—still, he managed to carry the caldron to the other end of the worktable, and holding his breath, to deposit it there. Then, with a sharp glance at the raven, he hurried away and leaned, panting, against the shelves on the farthest wall.

"Hurry up, will you! the bird snapped at him, and startled him into spilling wine over the desk.

Dr. Craven grimaced as he pulled back his hand, righted the decanter. This was no dream. And now—now one of his books, one of his priceless volumes, had been stained. He started to reach for it, but glancing around, seeing the raven's eyes fixed upon him, he abandoned the gesture and hastily finished pouring instead.

The bird had departed its perch and was hovering over the table, waiting for the caldron and its contents to grow cool.

Dr. Craven closed his eyes, frowned mightily. After a few moments he heard the raven plop to the edge of the caldron, heard—or thought he heard—its beak break the tension of a thickly scummed surface, heard a protracted gurgling and then a noisy gulp.

"Mmm," the raven said. "That wasn't so bad." And after a sly tilt of its head to acknowledge Dr. Craven's feeble groan, it set about consuming the remainder of the potion.

For the merest instant Dr. Craven had looked up; then he had closed his eyes again, clamping the lids together so tightly as to make them ache. It was not a posture he could long maintain. Moreover, the raven was now making ungodly choking and gagging noises. Dr. Craven was curious. He took a deep breath; then he opened his eyes.

The raven was staggering from one to the other side of the tabletop, bumping into this bit of apparatus, avoiding that, grasping hideously, flapping its wings wildly and to no effect whatsoever.

Dr. Craven gaped at it in utter amazement, seeing it stagger more and more drunkenly, hearing it emit more and more horrible sounds, until, coming at last to the very edge of the table, it let out one final shriek, then toppled backwards and plummeted out of sight. Its body thumped dully on the stone floor. Then—silence.

Slowly, hesitantly, Dr. Craven moved toward where the bird had fallen. But when he was in a position to see what had happened, he automatically turned away. He forced himself to turn back, to keep his eyes open, to lean forward and look.

And he found himself looking at a man's face—a familiar face, rising up to greet him. He froze, staring at the face, trying to remember where and when he had seen it before.

Dr. Adolphus Bedlo had by now managed to scramble to his feet. He smiled cordially at his host, bowed to him, and in the self-same voice that had so recently issued from the throat of the raven, said, "Good evening."

Straightening now, Dr. Craven nodded to him and said questioningly, "Dr.—?"

"Bedlo," the guest supplied. "We met in London several years ago." He waited a moment, then added, "At a sorcerer's convention; you recall it."

"Yes," Dr. Craven finally agreed. He did remember. And he was quite certain that he hadn't liked this squat and ugly little man, this beady eyed and flabby jowled intruder on his retirement. Nevertheless, he smiled at him.

Dr. Bedlo fairly beamed in return. "Well now," he huffed, "everything seems to have worked out just—" Dr. Bedlo's mouth remained open only long enough to let a tiny strangled sound escape from somewhere deep within his throat. His eyes, bulging from their sockets, swiveled disconnectedly up and down, left and right over his body. And his arms—the arms that he had attempted to raise in a gesture of satisfaction—

He had no arms. He had only wings. Two glossy black wings—those of the raven.

CHAPTER 3

"YOU BUNGLING idiot!" Dr. Bedlo's face contorted first with shock, then with rage. "Look what you've done to me!" He glared murderously at Dr. Craven.

"*I*" his hapless benefactor protested, and cringed back against the worktable.

"You made the potion, didn't you? Dr. Bedlo flapped at him with the only things available for flapping—two black wings, wings that now seemed stubby and absurdly, terrifyingly, small.

Dr. Craven remained silent, puzzled, miserable.

"Well," Dr. Bedlo insisted, "*do* something!"

"All I can do is—Dr. Craven shook his head. He didn't know what he could do. He was starting to edge along the table, away from Bedlo, away from the hideous wings, when his elbow jarred against a retort and sent it clattering on the stone floor. He stopped, and sitting heavily on one of the benches, he put his head in his hands and indulged in a moment's thought. "I can try to make some *more* potion," he suggested in a bravely shrill voice.

Dr. Bedlo turned from him in disgust, paced a few yards, then paced back and sank onto the other end of the same bench. Sighing, he said, "Well, make it then."

"Yes!" Dr. Craven twitched, and with a hasty glance at Bedlo, he stood up and set about measuring ingredients for the new potion. Hartshorn spirits: a vulture's tongue; bat's blood, dried; rabbit's lard; chain links from a gallows bird. He worked quickly and efficiently, dropping one after the other into the caldron, which he had now returned to its position over the lighted candles.

"What a night!" Dr. Bedlo said, mostly to himself. And reaching up as if to put his right hand over his eyes, he slapped himself with a wing. He glowered at the wing for a few moments; then, growling in fury, he flung it downward.

The eye of a white weasel had gone into the caldron, as had the proper quantity of jellied spiders, and now Dr. Craven reached for the box of dead man's hair. When he picked it up it felt strangely light—too light. He opened it and looked in. Then his face went blank.

Noticing that the chef had fallen idle, Dr. Bedlo sweetly and sarcastically asked, "What are you *waiting* for?"

Dr. Craven replied with a sick smile.

"What is it?" Dr. Bedlo asked in tones that had suddenly coarsened into those of threat.

"The—dead man's—hair?" Dr. Craven looked at him in open-mouthed defeat.

"What about it?"

"There"—Dr. Craven gulped painfully—there isn't any more."

"That's all I need, Dr. Bedlo said, fixing his host in a quiet stare. For an instant he seemed to be on the verge of smiling. Then, suddenly his face turned a volcanic purple, his eyes darkened with rage, his whole body quivered spasmodically; he shouted, "Well, get some more of it then!"

"*More?*" Dr. Craven recoiled. "Where?" he asked, afraid of the answer.

"In a *grave*yard!" Dr. Bedlo shrieked at him. "Where else?"

Dr. Craven was stunned. "Invade a graveyard at this time of night?" He shook his head. "Despoil the dead?"

"Would you rather I spent the rest of my life like *this?*" Dr. Bedlo asked, standing up now, and thrusting his wings toward the other man's face.

Dr. Craven's head was still shaking against the notion—the fear—of prying at caskets to deprive the resting dead of their hair. It was several moments before he could bring his eyes, and his mind, to focus on the wings. Those terrible wings! He gazed at them in uncomfortable indecision. He had always been a kindly man, generous, sympathetic, obliging. Surely, he could never allow anyone, even Bedlo, to go through life with black wings instead of arms. Yet graveyards, digging, caskets, corpses! He shuddered violently.

"*Would* you?" Dr. Bedlo shouted, suddenly afraid.

Dr. Craven relented. "No," he said quietly, and patted his rotund guest on the wing. "Let's be on our way."

"That won't be necessary," Dr. Craven answered unhappily. He had a feather in his fingers. Discreetly, he let it drop to the floor. "Father is in the—family crypt down here. Perhaps" —he nodded sadly, kicked at the feather with his foot—"Perhaps he wouldn't mind if we—took a snip or two. In a good cause."

At his host's gesture, Dr. Bedlo moved toward the door. Dr. Craven, catching sight of a dagger, picked it up. Then, after retrieving the candelabrum, he followed Dr. Bedlo out of the laboratory.

For several moments, the two men, who walked side by side down the stone corridor, heard only the thick echoes of their own footsteps. Then, clearing his throat, Dr. Craven ventured upon a topic that had been troubling him. "How—" He stopped, clearing his throat again, then continued.

"How did you come to find yourself in this—awkward state?"

"You have heard, I presume, of Dr. Scarabus," the other man answered easily.

"*Scarabus!*" Dr. Craven exclaimed. "Heaven help us, was *he* the one who did this to you?"

Dr. Bedlo gestured with a wing. "He's the one, all right."

Appalled, Dr. Craven had halted in his tracks to stare at Bedlo. Now, starting to walk again, he asked in tones that could scarcely conceal his agitation, "But how did this come about?"

"Well." Dr. Bedlo paused thinking. "I had been invited to his castle for dinner. I am a member of the United Brotherhood of Sorcerers—of which Scarabus is the Grand Master. You've heard of the Brotherhood?"

Dr. Craven nodded grimly. "My father was its Grand Master for twenty-seven years—with Scarabus his rival for power every minute of the time."

"I didn't know that, Dr. Bedlo said, surprised.

"Yes," his companion told him, "and it is precisely because of my painful memories of those years that I have never seen fit to join the Brotherhood.

"But if your father was the Grand Master, then, by direct line of ascension, you are entitled to claim the grand mastership for yourself."

"*Heaven forbid!* I prefer to practice my magic at home." Dr. Craven lapsed into silence, a kind of requiem silence for the powers he had once had—the powers he perhaps still had. Or did he? Could he now summon from his fingers anything more than prettily colored lines and idle shapes to trick his own mind away from its grief for Lenore? He wondered. And he decided it would be best not to wonder. Not now, at any rate. Some day—some day perhaps—when his spirit was a little easier—

He looked up, realizing that he had, without thinking turned a corner. He and Dr. Bedlo, who had fallen a few paces behind him, were now in a narrow subpassage, a dark tunnel that branched away from the main corridor and tended downward, into the dampness of the earth. Shuddering, he glanced around.

Yes, it was the right passage; in a moment it would lead to a flight of steps—and then to the crypt. He sighed, and his sigh was of disappointment as much, or more, than it was relief. A delay, any delay, would have been welcome. He motioned to Dr. Bedlo and waited for him to come again to his side.

Then he resumed his questioning of the other man. "You were telling me"—he stared pointedly at the place where Dr. Bedlo's arms should have been—"what happened to you."

"What?" Dr. Bedlo lifted a startled wing. "Oh," he said, recalling the momentarily forgotten problem. "Yes. Well, as I told you, I was invited to Scarabus' castle for dinner, and, uh—during the course of the meal, I—shall we say?—Partook a little overzealously of the wine. As a result of which I became somewhat—abusively critical of Scarabus' ability. Then—to top it all off—"

"Yes?" Dr. Craven urged him on.

"I challenged him to a duel."

"Of *magic?*" Dr. Craven asked aghast.

"It wasn't a fear contest," Dr. Bedlo said grumpily. "While I was endeavoring to implement my own magic—with the powders, potions, what have you—Scarabus was"—he gestured with his wings—"waving his fingers in the air—"

"You mean"—Dr. Craven interrupted shrilly, tremulously—"he only used *his hands?*"

"What of it?" Dr. Bedlo asked, puzzled by the shocked expression on his companion's face.

Before he answered, Dr. Craven paused to catch up the candelabrum, which had almost slipped away from him, then to readjust his grip on it—and so readjust his grip on himself. When he at last spoke, he did so in a slow and cautious voice, and he punctuated his every word with a fearful nod. "Then Scarabus' skill is far greater than I ever dreamed."

"What do you mean, greater?" Dr. Bedlo asked, starting to pout. "It was cheating."

"Oh no, Dr. Bedlo. Magic by gesture of hand is the most advanced of sorcery."

"I don't agree," Dr. Bedlo said, stubbornly emphatic. "If I'd have been sober, it would have been a different story."

Dr. Craven only shook his head despondently.

"Yes," Dr. Bedlo bristled, "it *would* have!"

They had now reached the stairs and had begun, in silence to descend.

When they were at the bottom of the flight, outside the door to the crypt, Dr. Bedlo, who could not let the subject rest, proclaimed in a sullen mutter, "Well, I'll get my revenge on that old monster."

Dr. Craven had turned his back and was searching along the wall for the key to the crypt door. He said nothing.

And Dr. Bedlo, piqued at this, snorted loudly, then growled, "See if I don't."

Dr. Craven whirled about. Holding the key, which he had found and taken from its hook, he stared intently at Bedlo, and he pleaded, "With all my heart, sir, I tell you this: *Do not go back there.*"

Then, as Dr. Bedlo frowned at him, he abruptly jammed the key into the lock, turned it, and shoved at the door which glided inward—opening so quickly and so noiselessly as to leave him gasping. He was off balance at first. And a moment later, he was rigid with anxiety. He stood before the vault, and he was afraid, afraid with a fear made all the more potent by his total inability to give it any explanation or to assign to it any cause.

Something brushed against his sleeve. He felt himself starting to cry out, and then, suddenly, he heard himself giggle instead. The something had been Dr. Bedlo—or, more properly, Dr. Bedlo's left wing. The fat little personage had simply shuffled past his host's side and gone into the crypt ahead of him. Now he stood in front of Dr. Craven, waiting for him to follow with the light.

This Dr. Craven did. Yet he was no less tense for his instant of angry relief. Beads of clammy sweat glittered on his forehead as he entered the grim and gloomy chamber, and holding the candelabrum rather lower than before, guided Dr. Bedlo along a wide aisle ranked on either side with granite platforms, each of which held a casket.

At last the two men reached that platform into which the name *Roderick Craven* had been chiseled, and the dates *1323-1396*.

Dr. Craven walked—hesitantly—into the space between it and the next platform. He gazed at his father's casket for a moment. Then, after setting the candelabrum on a nearby ledge, he lifted the dagger he had taken from the laboratory, slit the seal of the coffin, undid the twin iron hasps, and bracing himself, threw back the lid.

And now—now he could look down at—at Roderick Craven's corpse. He swallowed hard. Then he looked.

Roderick Craven's flesh lay waster and gray; dry, sunken, shriveled. Yet it was intact upon his bones. Beneath it, his features were well preserved; indeed, they were almost preternaturally distinct. His hair had matted and fallen over his wide brow. His lips, twisting upward at the corners, were set into an expression if—impatience? indignation? wrath? It was impossible to tell which.

"Well—" Erasmus Craven drew in a wavering breath. "Forgive me, Father," he said contritely. Then, bending close, he seized a portion of the matted hair, gently separated it from the locks to which it clung, and holding it up, began to saw at its roots with the edge of the dagger.

He had finished cutting off the hair and was about to turn away from the coffin when, suddenly, he petrified.

The fingers of the dead man's right hand were slowly flexing in. The hand was starting to rise.

Dr. Bedlo, whose view of the cadaver was obstructed by Erasmus Craven's back, glowered at that back, and asked crossly, "What are you waiting f—" He broke off as Dr. Craven dropped the dagger and the hair, made a hideous gagging sound, and shrank away from the casket.

Now both men stared, horrified, unable to move, at the hand—and now the arm—rising up from out of the casket.

Higher the hand came. And higher.

Suddenly, bony fingers clutched at Dr. Craven's neck. Sharp nails touched his skin. And he was being drawn down, toward the casket, his face toward the withered and ghastly face of his dead father.

He tried to pull free. But he couldn't. He was too weak; the hand was too strong. He whimpered feebly, insanely. Then he could make no sound at all.

The hand held him tight as, gasping in dumb terror, he saw the corpse's eyelids tremble and then, with shocking abruptness, jerk open.

Roderick Craven's eyes bored fiercely into those of this son. Roderick Craven's dead lips writhed apart, grinned at him. Roderick Craven's voice whispered harshly, hollowly, "Be-*ware-e-e-e!*"

Chapter 4

THE CORPSES'S eyes remained rigidly open for several seconds more. Then, in an instant, they shut again. The glaring pupils were gone; the trembling lids trembled no longer.

Dr. Craven gasped. Suddenly, he realized that he was free. The bony hand had released him and had settled back into the casket, where it rested now athwart the corpse's chest. One finger, the index finger, was still slightly flexed—as if its ragged and blackened nail had been temporarily enjoined to stop scratching at the collarbone of the dead. Dr. Craven giggled idiotically at the sight of it. He leaned in closer, looking at it. Then, abruptly, he reared back, recoiling from the casket in swift horror—and bumping into his friend Bedlo.

The two men gripped and clung to each other—Craven with his arms tight about Bedlo's waist, and Bedlo with his wings on Craven's shoulders, pressing up toward Craven's ears. And huddling thus, both men stared at the corpse, which was quiet once more. Indeed, except for the one finger, and except for the lock of hair that was noticeably missing from his forehead, Roderick Craven seemed never to have been disturbed at all.

"W-w-w-what did he say?" Dr. Bedlo asked, barely able to speak.

"H-he told me to *beware.*"

"Of what?"

"I don't know." Dr. Craven dropped his arms, shook his head in dumb amazement.

Dr. Bedlo had let his wings fall to his sides. He looked at Dr. Craven and swallowed dryly, clickingly; then he said, "Sh-shall we" —his voice cracked—"leave now?"

Dr. Craven swallowed too. Then, gingerly, he reached out, and holding himself as far away as possible, lowered the lid of the casket.

He hazed at it for a moment, and finally, picking up the candelabrum in a shaking hand, he started backing toward the door of the crypt.

"Don't forget the hair," Dr. Bedlo said weakly.

"Oh, yes." Dr. Craven stooped down and retrieved the hair and the dagger. Then the two men backed off toward the door, speeding their steps when they were halfway up the aisle that led to it, then, when they were but a little farther, turning and running out.

Breathing hard, and still trembling, Dr. Craven closed the door, pulled it tight, and locked it. The key, which he returned to its hook, swung back and forth against the wall, jangling noisily as the two men made their scampering way back to the laboratory.

Meanwhile, inside the crypt, behind the locked door, and under the closed lid of his coffin, Roderick Craven, deceased for twenty-two years, whispered again, harshly again, and hollowly, but almost so softly as not to be audible, "Be-*ware-e-e-e.*

And in the hours that followed, the hours between then and dawn, he whispered often, and always the same word, the same warning—which no one heeded. "Be-*ware-e-e-e!*"

Wine was what Dr. Bedlo usually wanted. Strong wine. And the more the better. Thus, just as soon as the black wings were gone and his arms and his hands were restored in good order to their previous and accustomed sites, wine was what Dr. Bedlo demanded.

Dr. Craven agreed readily.

Now the two men were once more in Dr. Craven's study and Dr. Craven, standing near the desk, was pouring. He gave the first glass to Dr. Bedlo, who downed its contents in a single concentrated gulp. Dr. Bedlo belched. Then, while his host sipped nervously, he helped himself to a second glass, the contents of which he made disappear as quickly and as noisily as he had those of the other.

As Dr. Craven settled wearily into the chair behind the desk, Dr. Bedlo, watching him, grabbed up the decanter and filled his glass for the third time. After he had taken a healthy swallow and a glance, sideways now and perhaps a trifle bleary, at Dr. Craven, he lowered himself into a nearby chair and proceeded, glass in hand, to remark, "Rather unexpected—what happened down there."

"Most unexpected," Dr. Craven agreed with a tired and tremulous nod. "Why should he return from the dead? To tell me to beware?"

"I wish I knew," Dr. Bedlo said, and finishing his wine, he reached forward, set the empty glass on the desk. "However—it's time for me to be getting back to the castle of Dr. Scarabus."

Dr. Craven jolted up in his chair. "Sir," he said in a voice made hoarse by distress, "I implore you." He leaned toward Dr. Bedlo, stared at him, extended to him an open palm and fingers tensed with entreaty. *"Stay away from Scarabus."*

"Impossible," Dr. Bedlo answered stubbornly. "He confiscated all my magical equipment. I want it back." Dr. Bedlo paused to grin foolishly into Dr. Craven's earnest stare. Then, with a great frown, he pounded his fist on the desk, and added, "And I want revenge."

"But he is too *powerful,*" Dr. Craven protested.

"Go with me then," Dr. Bedlo said, beaming with sudden inspiration.

"What?" Dr. Craven was horrified.

"Together we would be more than a match for him."

"No, sir. *Never.* I want nothing to do with him. Nothing at all."

"Oh," Dr. Bedlo said glumly, and the radiance, the hope, was gone from his face. He slumped disconsolately in his chair for a moment. Then, leaning forward and starting to pick up his wineglass, he noticed an oil miniature standing in a gold frame on the near side of the desk.

His hand automatically took up the wineglass, but only to hold it for an instant and then, very abruptly, to put it down again, to seize the portrait, and to bring it close to his eyes so that he could better stare at it.

At last, he looked from the miniature to Dr. Craven, who had been blinking at him in surprise. "What are you doing with a painting of this woman?" he asked, turning the portrait around to expose it to Dr. Craven's view.

"She was my *wife* sir."

"Left you anh?" Dr. Bedlo said with a quasi-sympathetic shrug.

"Certainly now." Erasmus Craven's tone made it abundantly clear that he was offended. He glanced toward the doors to the chapel, returned his gaze to the portrait of Lenore, and sighed heavily—heartbrokenly.

He was in the midst of a second sigh when Dr. Bedlo asked, "Then what is she doing in Dr. Scarabus's castle?"

"*What!*" Choking slightly, Dr. Craven gasped out the word. He was thunderstruck, and for several moments, could say no more. He glowered at Dr. Bedlo; then, when he had somewhat recovered himself, he declared emphatically, "This is impossible, sir. She has been dead for more than two years."

"I don't understand," Dr. Bedlo said, and setting the portrait back on the desk, he began to scratch his puzzled head.

Suddenly, Dr. Craven didn't understand either. He glanced once more at the chapel doors. He was uncertain now, and he was beginning to be afraid in a completely new way. He turned again to Dr. Bedlo. "You still maintain that—"

"I'm *telling* you, Dr. Bedlo interrupted. "*This*"— he pointed at the portrait—"is the woman I saw at Dr. Scarabus' castle."

"*When?*"

"This *evening!*" Dr. Bedlo answered shrilly.

"No." Dr. Craven drew back, unwilling to accept this. Then, staring at Dr. Bedlo, he repeated loudly, as if to convince himself, "*No!*"

Shaking his head, Dr. Bedlo stayed silent. He watched Dr. Craven rise painfully from his chair, watched him lean against the desk for a moment, breathing in tortured gasps. He saw the wildness, and the desperation, in Dr. Craven's eyes, and then, saw him race across the study, jerk open the chapel doors, and lurch through them toward—?

By the time Dr. Bedlo was on his feet and in the open doorway, Dr. Craven was already at the altar. And by the time Dr. Bedlo had moved down the aisle to stand behind him, he had seized the candles and set them on the floor, torn the heavy purple cloth from the altar—and revealed it to be a casket.

Dr. Craven was clawing at the seal, undoing the hasps, and at last, flinging up the lid.

And now both men flinched, and both turned pale.

In the coffin was a woman's body. The face was to desiccated to be recognizable. But the hair was black—jet black, like that of Lenore.

Dr. Craven turned agitatedly to the other man, who was staring at the corpse in total bewilderment. *"Well?* Dr. Craven asked.

"I—I don't understand," Dr. Bedlo stammered. "I— *swear* to you—I—I *saw* her there! I *saw* her there this very evening!"

"No!" Dr. Craven gripped Bedlo by the shoulders; he glared down at him, shook him violently, over and over. *"You saw someone else."*

Nevertheless, Dr. Bedlo insisted, "I saw *her!"* And twisting himself partially away from his enraged host, he pointed at the large oval portrait above the casket. *"Her!" he shouted.* "Her!"

Dr. Craven looked at him in stunned silence; he looked at the portrait; then he dropped his hands. "How can this be?" he asked, horrified. *"Unless—"*

"What?"

"Unless Scarabus has gained control of her spirit."

"You mean it was a *ghost* I saw?" Dr. Bedlo grimaced as he considered this possibility. "But"—he shook his head—why should Scarabus want to do—"

Before Dr. Bedlo could finish, Erasmus Craven had supplied the answer, *"To take his revenge on the house of Craven."* He paused for a moment. Then he announced grimly, "This profanation must be *ended."*

"You mean you'll go *with* me?" Despite everything, Dr. Bedlo seemed almost elated.

Dr. Craven gazed upward, first at the portrait of Lenore, then toward heaven. He clapped his hand over his heart, and without bothering to look down, far down, at little Dr. Bedlo, he told him, "For the sake of Lenore's tormented soul—I *must* go with you.

Chapter 5

THE BELLCORD had been pulled, tugged, jerked almost from its moorings. Now Dr. Craven, on his knees in front of the study fireplace, was stirring at the half expired embers with a thick iron poker, blowing mightily on them, pumping a leather bellows under the grate. Whenever he could develop enough flames to make it feasible, he added a log from the pile that was beside him on the vast stone hearth.

Dr. Bedlo leaned against the chapel doors, which had once again been closed. He smiled to himself as he watched the feverish labors of his host. There was a wineglass in his hand, and when he wasn't sipping, or gulping, he softly hummed a chantlike little tune.

He was surprised when Dr. Craven suddenly stood and faced about. But Dr. Craven had turned, not to him, but to the hallway door, opening now to admit the brutish figure of Grimes, the Cravens' coachman.

Grimes stood at attention, albeit at rather sleepy attention. "Yes, sir," he said, and waited for Dr. Craven to give him his instructions.

"Prepare the carriage for immediate departure."

"Yes, sir," Grimes said obediently. Then he hurried off to do as he had been told.

Dr. Bedlo, who had put down his wineglass and moved closer to his host, rubbing his hands before the newly made fire and grinned after the departing coachman with unconcealed delight. Dr. Bedlo looked forward to the coming journey. Naively, he looked forward to obtaining his revenge—whatever that might be.

Dr. Craven stared at him for a long moment. He frowned at him. And then he sighed resignedly—and determinedly, and nobly. Motioning him toward the still open hallway door, he suggested in a soft, almost paternal tone, "You'll need something to protect you from the cold."

"Yes, Yes, indeed." Dr. Bedlo literally bounced across the study and through the door.

Dr. Craven followed him out, then guided him into the large entry hall, where he stopped before a tall wooden cabinet, tugged open its twin doors, and after checking, took out a cloak and hat. "Try these," he said, and helped his guest on with the cloak.

It was many sizes too big, sagging onto the floor in an unintended and absurd train. Dr. Bedlo looked down at it, then up as Dr. Craven handed him the hat. It fit horribly, drooping over Dr. Bedlo's ears, covering his eyebrows, and all but covering his eyes. From beneath it, he gazed at Dr. Craven.

Neither man said a word.

Estelle Craven, usually a sound sleeper, had awakened suddenly. For what reason she didn't know. Sitting up in bed, she had stared about her, seen nothing. Then she had risen, and in her bare feet, run to one of the windows which looked out over the rear of the house.

On the ground near the stable there was a small candelabrum, its lights dwarfed and flickering eerily in the night wind. And outside the stable doors there was a man—a gigantic man. Without seeing his face, Estelle knew at once that this man could be non other than Grimes.

She peered out at him, and to her surprise, saw that his arms were lifted, but motionless—as if his hands had somehow gotten stuck to the highest of the three latches that held the stable doors in place. Then, with a gasp, she realized that not only were his arms motionless, his whole body was motionless, rigid, seemingly frozen into a pose, and an awkward and uncomfortable pose, at that.

Estelle rubbed her eyes. She blinked. She looked away into the darkness and identified the outline of a familiar hill, a familiar tree, a familiar clump of shrubs. Then she looked back at Grimes—he was exactly as she had seen him first.

And for many moments, long moments, he remained so. The wind shrieked insanely during those moments, and the sky became mottled and took on an unhealthy purplish cast. The candelabrum toppled over, and all of its lights went out.

But Grimes did not stir.

Then there was a flash of lightning—or at least, what Estelle thought was lightning—and followed it, an abrupt and total silence. Grimes lurched drunkenly. He fell against the wall of the stable, picked himself up, and then, reeling, turned around and stood swaying dizzily on his feet.

Estelle stifled a scream as a dull red spot seemed to appear in the center of Grime's forehead, and got larger and brighter, and assumed a strange, crablike form that seared into his skull—and then was gone.

With her fist clenched up to her mouth, her teeth biting hard on a tensed and whitened knuckle, she watched the coachman stop swaying, stand erect to the full limit of his enormous height, and march—yes, march—off in the direction of the house. As he disappeared from her view she heard a weird hissing noise. This, she told herself—this, if nothing else—was surely a trick of the wind, and of the storm that was now clotting the heavens and threatening on the instant to explode.

Three hats were stacked one on top of the other on the large table in the entrance hall. Dr. Bedlo added a fourth, and then took from Dr. Craven, who was now wearing his own cloak and hat, still one more. Like its predecessors, it proved to be far to capacious for Dr. Bedlo's plump knob of a head. It looked ridiculous.

Dr. Bedlo was grimacing, shrugging, holding up his hands in a gesture of despair, when Estelle Craven called from the staircase at the rear of the hall, "Father?"

Both men turned to the sound of her voice.

"You're going out at this hour?" She gazed questionly from her father to Dr. Bedlo. Then, as both approached the staircase, she fixed her eyes on Dr. Craven.

"Yes, my dear," he told her, nodding calmly, and then, after he had reached the foot of the steps, smiling up at her.

She frowned worriedly in return. Starting to say something, she changed her mind, frowned again, and modesly pulling the wrapper tighter about her night clothes, hurried downstairs to confront her father and his unknown guest.

Dr. Craven gave her his arm as she alighted from the bottom step. "This is Dr. Bedlo," he said to her, motioning with his free hand.

And to Dr. Bedlo, he presented, "My daughter, Estelle."

"Charmed," Dr. Bedlo said, sweeping the outsized hat from his head as he paid this beautiful young girl the compliment of his very deepest bow.

"Dr. Bedlo," Estelle acknowledged him distractedly. Then she turned away, and letting go of Dr. Craven's arm, moved back a pace to look at him and ask, "Where are you going, Father?"

"I cannot tell you, my dear," he said, averting his eyes as he spoke.

And now Estelle was truly anxious. She waited for him to say more. But he didn't. And he very carefully kept his eyes from meeting hers.

At last, taking a deep breath to prepare herself for his reply, she asked in a voice trembling with fear of what that reply might be, "It's something dangerous, isn't it?"

"*No*" he said, and she knew that he was lying. Yet how could she contradict him? What could she do?

He turned to Dr. Bedlo and was saying, "Shall we go, sir?"

Suddenly, Estelle knew what she could do. "I'm going with you," she declared.

"You—!" Dr. Craven was shocked. Now he looked at her, glared fiercely at her, and with all the authority that his exasperation and worry would allow him to command, told her, "You most certainly are *not!*"

Before she could protest he had started toward the door, signaling Dr. Bedlo to come with him.

Dr. Bedlo, however, deemed it essential to take his proper leave of Estelle, pay her his proper respects. Once more he swept back the hat and bowed from his waist. "A pleasure to meet you, my dear," he murmured.

Estelle, momentarily stunned, said nothing.

Her father was halfway to the door. She started after him, then stopped, waited. He was returning. Soon, he had his arm around her shoulder. "Now you're not to concern yourself, Estelle," he said. "I can't tell you where I'll be but—rest assured I'll be perfectly all right." Guiding her along with his arm, with the soft pats and the gentle pressure of his hand against her back, he walked to the door.

Not until he reached it did he release her. Then, glancing into her eyes, which were moist with tears, he bent to kiss her goodby.

Dr. Bedlo, who had joined them, smiled. "Don't worry your pretty head, my dear," he told her. "Nothing bad is going to happen."

No sooner had these words been uttered than the door flew open—crashing into Dr. Craven's side and impelling him violently backward, away from Estelle and toward one of the great wooden columns that were spaced along the walls of the entry hall to give added support to the roof.

Estelle screamed.

At that same moment, Dr. Craven stumbled, and hitting the column head-on, sagged to the floor. Dr. Bedlo hoisted his trailing cloak and looked desperately this way and that, seeking cover. And the cold night wind rushed into the hall, blowing the hats off the table and extinguishing all of the candles in their sconces.

Now the hall was lighted only by the two small candelabra that stood on iron legs at either side of the door.

There was enough light to glint off the blade of a huge ax, viciously upraised. And there was enough light to show that Grimes, who was holding the ax, was clearly in the throes of some incredible mania, that his eyes glittered insanely, that his lips were drawn back from clenching teeth and that his steps as he advanced were mechanical and grotesquely deliberate.

Breathing in quick, panting hisses, Grimes moved forward, into the hall.

Estelle and Dr. Bedlo backed off, slowed by confusion, slowed by terror.

And Grimes came closer.

Suddenly, he stopped, as did they. He glanced at them for a moment. Then he grunted hideously, and the ax tore downward. Estelle screamed again, and as she and Dr. Bedlo lunged in opposite directions, the ax blade buried itself in the floor between them.

Snarling now, Grimes jerked at the instrument, freed it; then, lifting it to his shoulder, he looked around wildly—and saw Dr. Bedlo running toward the stairs, then catching his feet in the hem of the too long cloak, and in consequence, sprawling across the bottom step.

The coachman swung his ax through the air as if to test it. Grinning crazily, he hefted it back to his shoulder, looked at the fallen Dr. Bedlo, and strode across the hall in the direction of the stairs.

Estelle gasped. Then, seeing Grimes move away, she ran to her father and knelt beside him. He was half sitting, half lying against the column, and when she touched him, he only swayed slightly, then returned to his original position. *Father,"* she called frightenedly.

A dazed smile came to his lips, and he opened his eyes. But he was staring straight ahead, blankly, smiling at nothing. Estelle was about to shake him, when she heard Dr. Bedlo shriek, *"No!"*

Gasping again, she looked toward the stairway. And then she screamed. Over and over, she screamed.

Dr. Bedlo was clambering up the steps on his hands and knees, losing time as he pulled the cloak behind him, losing time as his feet were ensnared by its dragging bulk, losing time as every second he goggled backward at Grimes—and at the ax, which was now poised high, waiting to descend.

"Get away from me, you ugly brute," Dr. Bedlo shouted, and then, turning, he clambered up one more step.

The coachman took two, then another, and another, and then in a single stride, four more. His lips writhed into a maniacal grin. And the ax blade crashed down, just missing Dr. Bedlo, but biting through the folds of his cloak.

The cloak, and Dr. Bedlo with it, were now pinned to the stairs. Dr. Bedlo was trying desperately to crawl from under it, but he couldn't. Grimes, who had backed down several steps, was bent over, trying to untangle and dislodge the ax blade, and he was having as little success with this project as Dr. Bedlo was having with his efforts to escape from beneath the cloak.

At last, Grimes, grunting, detached the blade from its handle.

And in the same instant, Dr. Bedlo, whining, twisted open the catch of the cloak.

Grimes gripped the handle as he would a bludgeon. He snorted in what appeared to be satisfaction with the new weapon. Then, holding it ready, he began once more to stalk Dr. Bedlo.

But the intended victim, loose from the cloak that had restrained him, had managed to scramble to his unsteady feet. Now he was moving up the steps again, supporting himself by clutching hand over hand at the baluster rail. Indeed, he had almost gained the top of the flight.

Grimes was far below, near the bottom. He hurried after Dr. Bedlo—too fast. For, as he swung at Dr. Bedlo—and missed him—he lost his balance. Tottering crazily, he dropped the ax handle, which bounced down the stairs, clattering against the balusters on its way. A moment later, despite the wild pumping and circling of his hands and arms, or perhaps because of it, Grimes toppled backward.

He crashed to the floor of the entry hall, groaned once, rolled over, and then was heard no more.

Dr. Bedlo took a series of deep breaths. He gazed down at Grimes and sighed. Then, squaring his shoulders and giving his head a slight but distinctly vain tilt, he came strutting to the bottom of the stairs.

Pausing only long enough to nudge Grimes with the tip of his foot, and to smirk when Grimes showed no reaction, he hastened over to Estelle, who was still on her knees beside Dr. Craven. She was chafing at his wrists now, trying to bring him back to consciousness. And he was still staring forward, smiling blankly, foolishly, not moving.

"What's the matter with him?" Dr. Bedlo asked, suddenly alarmed. .

"He must have struck his head," Estelle said, looking up as she went on with her work.

Dr. Bedlo watched her for a moment. Then, stooping at Dr. Craven's other side, he bellowed into his ear, "*Wake up Erasmus!*"

It was no use.

"You've got to *do* something!" Dr. Bedlo whined at Estelle.

"Can't *you* do something!" she asked.

"Not without my magical equipment." He held out his hands to her and shrugged slowly, mournfully. Then, standing, he gazed about him, as if the magical equipment might magically appear.

What he saw was Grimes. Grimes—who had somehow risen. Grimes—who had somehow gotten the ax blade loose and somehow reunited it with its handle. Grimes—who was coming toward him.

And what he did was run, heading for the open door just as fast as his short little legs could carry him.

Gasping, Estelle jerked her head around and watched him go.

"Dr. Bedlo!" she called after him in surprise. And now she, too, saw Grimes. "Dr. Bedlo! she called again, this time in mortal terror. "Don't leave us!"

He paused in the doorway, but only long enough to shout, "It's every man for himself, my dear!" Then he disappeared into the night.

"Father!" Estelle cried desperately, and started to shake the still sleeping, still smiling Dr. Craven. "Wake *up!*" She shook him harder, screamed at him, *"Father!"*

Grimes was getting closer. His huge form was looming almost overhead. He raised the ax.

Estelle screamed, *"No!"* She scrambled to her feet, tugged at her father, trying to pull him from Grimes' path.

And now Grimes was upon her. Roughly, he shoved her aside, lowering the ax to do it. Then, lifting the ax again, he swung with all his might at Dr. Craven, who smiling the while, slumped over—and thereby avoided the blade, which dug into the column in precisely that spot where his head had rested an instant before.

As Grimes lunged for the ax handle—and Dr. Craven slumbered blissfully on the floor—Estelle ran to a nearby table and seized from it a large vase. Then, with the vase in her hands, she ran back, reaching Grimes just as he had wrenched the ax from out of the column.

He bent down, starting to position the weapon for another swing at Dr. Craven. He didn't see Estelle. And she, coming upon him from behind, smashed the vase over the top of his skull.

For a moment, the coachman remained motionless. There were shards of the vase on his shoulders, shards in his hair, and shards scattered on the floor at his feet. At last, blinking, he shook himself, and as the fragments of pottery tumbled from him, he straightened and turned to face Estelle.

Sobbing, she backed away.

Once more, Grimes raised his ax/ And as Estelle retreated, her eyes wide in terror, he followed. He walked slowly, glaring at her, waiting for her to be trapped against the wall toward which she was backing.

Suddenly, Estelle realized what was happening. She screamed, and gasping, she jumped aside. But Grimes moved with her. He cut her off as she tried to dodge past him; then he started to advance again, started to force her to the wall.

Dr. Bedlo had returned to stand in the comparative safety of the doorway. He was watching, but keeping himself set to run again should necessity—or wisdom—so dictate. Now he covered his eyes with his hands, and peeking from between his spread fingers, muttered softly, "I can't bear to look."

And now Estelle was against the wall. She could do nothing—nothing but scream. And scream she did—so loudly and so shrilly that her father grumbled in his sleep, and closing his eyes, rolled over to sleep on his other side.

Chapter 6

ALL OF a sudden, Erasmus Craven started violently. Once more, he rolled over. Then, opening his eyes, he sat up and looked around.

A moment later he was on his feet, wide awake, alert to his daughter's peril.

He slapped at his temple—hard—and knew that the sure knowledge was in his brain, just where it had always been. The magic was available. The power was in his fingertips ready to surge forth. Staring at the coachman, he raised his right hand in a dramatic gesture.

Grimes was snarling, and his ax, having come to its highest point, was beginning to descend upon Estelle.

A kind of white lightning crackled in Dr. Craven's palm and along the length of his fingers. Then, shooting out, it became a single bolt—which bounced off the back of the coachman's skull at the very instant of the ax's swiftest falling.

With a grunt of brute pain, Grimes whirled about, dazed. The ax was still tight in his hands, making him stagger insanely under the burden of its accumulated momentum. He lurched this way, reeled that, and finally, pulled forward by the ax, he collapsed in front of the doorway—and almost on top of Dr. Bedlo.

As Dr. Craven hurried to embrace Estelle, Dr. Bedlo quietly closed the door. Then, stepping around the fallen Grimes, he moved a little farther into the hall, stopped, turned, and proceeded to stare at the coachman in open-mouthed awe.

Estelle leaned weakly against her father.

"Are you all right, my dear?" he asked.

She nodded, unable to speak.

Dr. Bedlo was nodding also, nodding in amazement, in wonder. "How did you do it?" he asked, walking toward Dr. Craven.

"Nothing worthy of note, sir," Dr. Craven said distractedly.

"Not worthy of *note?*" Dr. Bedlo was incredulous. "It was *fantastic.* I never saw—" He broke off as Estelle looked accusingly at him. Dropping his eyes, he tried to think of something to say to her, some excuse—any excuse.

Estelle, however, was looking at the coachman. Suddenly, she caught her breath, and recoiling against her father, clung to him in terror.

Grimes was stirring. His eyes were open, and he was starting to sit up. He moaned. Then, getting to his knees, he blinked at Dr. Craven and asked mildly, "What happened, sir?"

"What *happened?*" Dr. Bedlo fairly shouted. His face was red with fury, his whole body quivering and twitching with righteous indignation as he turned to glare at Grimes. "Why, you maniac, you!"

"Sir?" Grimes asked, blinking now at Dr. Bedlo, who had begun to shake his fist at him—and at the same time, to move back from him, toward Dr. Craven and the protection he could, if necessary, provide.

"What *did* happen, Grimes?" Dr. Craven asked after he had motioned Bedlo to be silent. He was curious. Why had the coachman attacked? Who, or what, had made him behave as he did?

"Well, sir." Grimes stood groggily, thought for a moment. "I was just about to enter the stable, and—" He stopped, suddenly confused. "How did I get in here?"

"You don't remember coming in?" Dr. Craven said, prompting him.

"No, sir. The last thing I recall is"—he touched his forehead, looked perplexed—"something—burning at my—head."

Dr. Craven gasped. No longer was he curious. He knew—knew what he had suspected, knew what he had feared.

"Burning?" Estelle asked, thinking now of the scene she had witnessed from her bedroom window.

"Never mind, Grimes," Dr. Craven said hastily. "It's not important. Prepare the coach."

Dr. Bedlo protested, "What do you mean, it's not important? He tried to—"

"No," Dr. Craven interrupted, holding up a hand to warn Bedlo not to continue.

Dr. Bedlo spluttered into silence.

And Dr. Craven—when he was quite assured of that silence—turned to the coachman and said firmly, "You may *go* now, Grimes."

"Yes, sir," Grimes answered, docile and obedient, albeit very, very confused. Then, walking slowly, with dazed eyes and tentative steps, he moved toward the archway that led to the rear of the house.

Dr. Bedlo's eyes bulged slightly, and his face was ruddy with amazement. "You're letting him *go?*"

Dr. Craven waited until the servant had disappeared. Then turning back to Adolphus Bedlo—guest, fellow sorcerer, and erstwhile raven—he said, "Can't you see that he has no idea what happened? Clearly, he was the victim of some diabolic mind control."

Dr. Bedlo was stunned. His eyes bulged farther from their sockets, but his face grew suddenly pale—and paler yet, almost ashen, as he considered the subject of mind control, how and by whom it might be exercised. At last he managed to gasp, *Scarabus?*"

"*Scarabus?*" Estelle echoed. It was a name well known, a name to fear. Estelle was still clinging to her father. She held him a little tighter as she asked, "Father, what has *he* to do with this?"

Dr. Craven patted her shoulder. He thought for a moment that he could evade the question. Then, realizing that he could not, he said gently, "It is to his castle that I must go, Estelle."

Estelle gazed up at her father in dismay. Then, stepping back from him, she looked at him again and said determinedly, "I'm going with you." And to cut off any argument, she added, "Would you leave me here alone after what just happened?"

Neither choice appealed to Dr. Craven. Estelle would be in danger if she came with him, in danger if she didn't—but possibly in greater danger if she was outside the sphere of his magic. Once more, he wondered about his powers. He knew now that he still possessed at least some of them. Hadn't he halted the coachman? Hadn't he freed him from Scarabus' spell? But what exact powers did he have? And how strong were they? Could he, for instance, protect Estelle from Scarabus if Estelle was alone and out of his sight. He wasn't sure.

The uncertainty, the fear, the need to make a decision, an immediate decision—all of this reflected on Erasmus Craven's face as pain. Dr. Bedlo looked at him worriedly. Estelle anxiously, and with pity for his dilemma.

At last, nodding unhappily, her told her, "Very well, my dear."

Estelle watched her for a moment, then protested to his host, "You're going to—?"

Dr. Craven shrugged despairingly.

Whereupon Dr. Bedlo, waiting until Estelle was near the stairway and thus out of hearing, protested again, more strongly now, in an outraged tone, and with the added emphasis of his of his waving hands. "This is madness, Dr. Craven! That helpless girl exposed to Dr. Scarabus?"

"What other choice *have* I?" Dr. Craven asked. "Can I leave her *here*—defenseless? What if Scarabus attacks again?"

Dr. Bedlo stopped short. He sighed and looked about him. Then, very disturbed, he asked, "You really think it was *he* who—"

"*Who else?*" Dr. Craven stared at the other man for a moment, hoping he could make some suggestion, but knowing that he could not. Then he continued, "Obviously, Scarabus knows that we are coming and does not mean for us to do so." He shuddered. "I never realized before just how dangerous a man Scarabus is."

Together Dr. Craven and Dr. Bedlo began to pace the floor. There was nothing more to be said, little more to be done. Dr. Craven relighted a few of the candles that had blown out when the coachman entered; he picked up the hats, those that had blown from the table and also the one Dr. Bedlo had been wearing, which had fallen to the floor when Bedlo first hoisted his borrowed cloak and ran; he retrieved that cloak from its place of abandonment on the stairs, and he retrieved the ax from in front of the doorway where Grimes had dropped and forgotten it. After he had put these things out of sight, he helped Dr. Bedlo select another cloak and another hat, both of which were of somewhat better fit than their predecessors had been—although neither was by any means small enough not to look a trifle absurd.

He had just found his own hat—it was near the column that had first induced, and afterwards supported him in his slumber—and he was beginning to brush off the nap and smooth the wide brim back into shape when Estelle started gliding down the steps. She was wearing a deep blue cloak the color of which intensified the lighter and clearer blue of her eyes. He head was uncovered, and her pale blond hair tumbled appealing on her shoulders. She looked very young—far younger than her nineteen years—very beautiful, and very, very frail.

As Dr. Craven moved toward the stairs to meet her, Dr. Bedlo seized his arm. held him back. "You're certain," Dr. Bedlo asked, "absolutely certain you won't reconsider?"

"I see no other way, sir," Dr. Craven told him, and after freeing his arm from Dr. Bedlo's restraining grip, he gestured him to the door with one hand, then extended the other to Estelle.

The three prospective travelers, walked to the door in silence. All three were gloomy, all were fearful, and all were grimly determined. Only Estelle, however, could manage to hide any of these feelings. She smiled up at her father in the same way she would have smiled if they had been setting out for a pleasant ramble in the woods.

She was still smiling when he held open the door for her. And when she started through it. Then, suddenly, she recoiled with a gasp.

Someone—a man—was standing on the doorstep, right arm raised as if to strike.

For several moments—during which Estelle recovered herself enough to note that he was handsome and quite young, older than she was, but not by more than two or three years—the man remained just as Estelle had first seen him. His arm stayed up in the air, his mouth open, and his eyes wide with surprise. He seemed not to be breathing.

Then Dr. Bedlo stepped up to him and asked crossly, "What are *you* doing here?"

"I've been looking for you, Father," Rexford Bedlo said, coming quickly to life.

And now several moments were elapsed, long moments, awkwardly silent. Dr. Bedlo stared at his son. His son stared at him, then at Estelle, whom he found extraordinarily pretty, then back at Dr. Bedlo. Estelle and her father, embarrassed, kept their eyes on the floor.

Finally, Dr. Bedlo, waving a hand toward the door, said to them, "This is Rexford." And to his son, "Dr. Craven and his daughter,

Estelle."

Coming inside, Rexford bowed to Estelle, whose glance he managed to catch and hold for a far to fleeting second. Then, as she smiled wanly at him, he said, "I apologize for startling you."

Estelle nodded and smiled again.

Rexford bowed to her father. "Doctor."

Her father returned the bow—rather perfunctorily, Estelle thought. "Sir."

And Dr. Bedlo, impatient, attempted to put an end to this nonsense by taking his son's shoulder, giving it a slight shove in the direction of the open door, and saying, "All right, you have to go now. We're in a hurry."

"But"—Rexford Bedlo stood his ground—"What about mother?"

"What about her?" Dr. Bedlo asked, bristling.

"She wants you home, Father." Rexford smiled clumsily at Estelle. He hated to discuss family problems in front of her and her father. Nevertheless, he had been compelled to do so.

"Well!" Dr. Bedlo huffed. Then, red-faced and furious he shouted, "She'll just have to wait! I have important business to transact!" He stamped his foot petulantly; then he gave his son a really vigorous push. *"Out of my way."*

Respectfully, but firmly, Rexford took hold of his father's arm. He meant Dr. Bedlo to come home with him.

Dr. Bedlo glared up at his son, so much taller, and so much stronger than he. He smiled, murderously at him, and then he whined, "Don't *do* that, Rexford."

"I'm sorry, Father, but"—embarrassed, Rexford lowered his voice almost to a whisper—mother gave me strict orders not to let you out of my sight once I'd found you."

"Well! Once more, Dr. Bedlo exploded. "You can tell old battle-ax to—!"

"Sir!" Dr. Craven cut him off. He stared warningly at him, waited for him to subside, then said, "We *must* be on our way."

"By all means." Dr. Bedlo glowered at his son. He tried to pull loose; failed. Tried harder; failed again. Now he was clearly verging on apoplexy—face shading from red to purple, eyes bulging and bloodshot, muscles atwitch. Still, he managed from between clenched

teeth to hiss, "If you don't stop that, Rexford, I'm going to smash you one right in your face."

Attempting to mediate, Dr. Craven took a strong grip on Rexford's arm. "Please, sir," he said, pressing that arm to show that he could move it if necessary, "I beg of you. We must *go.*"

Rexford looked at him, confused. And then Rexford looked at Estelle. Following which, Rexford decided. "Then I will go *with* you, sir."

"Certainly!" Dr. Bedlo spluttered. He was free now. Free to wave his arms in the air as he ranted. "Why not? Let's make it a family outing! Rexford, you must have some friends you'd like to bring along! Maybe you'd like to pick up your mother on the way! I'm sure Dr. Scarabus would love to have her!:

"Dr. Scarabus?" Rexford said, taken aback. He, too, knew the name—and feared it.

Dr. Bedlo answered him with a snarl of fury. Then, pushing past him, he lurched through the door and outside.

Rexford watched him go. Then, puzzled, he turned to Dr. Craven and waited for him to explain.

But Dr. Craven had no time for explanations—or for arguments. "Very well, sir," he said briskly. Come along then." And taking Estelle's arm, he guided her out, leaving a dazed and startled Rexford standing motionless in the open door.

Chapter 7

A TEAM of restless bays stomped impatiently in front of the Craven's carriage, which was ready and waiting in the drive. Grimes, enveloped in a sheepskin and calmly puffing at his pipe, sat high on the box, holding the animals in rein. And a few paces back, Dr. Adolphus Bedlo stood in the shadows and gazed warily at him.

Dr. Bedlo turned partially as he was joined by Dr. Craven and Estelle, and then by Rexford, who was panting and out of breath from the effort of catching up. With a covert nod of his head to indicate Grimes, the villain and brute, the good Dr. Bedlo hissed to his good friend Craven, "You're not going to let *him* drive us there, are you?"

"I don't like it," Dr. Craven answered. "But—if he stays here, who will—? He gestured toward the driver's box, then gave his shoulders a questioning shrug.

"I'll be glad to drive, sir," Rexford Bedlo submitted. Adolphus Bedlo had curled a lip to sneer at the boy. The mission would be—was perilous enough without this sort of thing getting in the way. With it—?

He looked from one to the other Bedlo. Best not to complicate matters, he thought; best not to issue futile warnings. And turning silently, he moved toward the carriage and called up to the man on the box, "Come down, Grimes."

Then, when the coachman had done so and was standing before him, he said, "You're to stay here."

"Sir?" Grimes asked, puzzled.

"And put that horse up for the night." Dr. Craven pointed to Rexford Bedlo's mare, which was tethered near the door of the house.

"Yes, sir," Grimes said meekly, and lumbered off to obey.

Rexford Bedlo had opened the carriage door and was holding it, waiting for the passengers to take their places. Nodding at him once more, Dr. Craven gestured Estelle toward the step.

But Estelle had other ideas. She touched her father's arm. Then, looking at the driver's seat, she said, "I'll ride up there Father. You know how ill it makes me to sit inside."

"Very well, my dear," he answered absently. Then he turned to the other passenger. "Dr. Bedlo?"

As the elder Bedlo started to get into the coach, Rexford tried to lend him a hand. Dr. Bedlo brushed that hand away. He snarled, *"I can manage by myself, thank you."* And then, pushing irritably at Rexford, he stumbled on the step, slipped, fell—and went sprawling, plump and ungainly and sputtering curses, onto the floor of the coach.

When Dr. Craven had been duly assisted in, Rexford shut the door of the coach, climbed lithely to the driver's seat, and reaching down, helped Estelle to her place beside him. He checked below, smiled at Estelle, and then picked up the reins and cracked the whip over the horses' heads—too hard. The coach jolted forward.

And inside, Dr. Bedlo lurched forward with it, toppled against Dr. Craven's knees, and finally, with a lout thump, sat down on the floor. *"I'll be glad to drive, sir,"* he said savagely, mimicking Rexford. Then, after Dr. Craven had helped him up, he looked across his shoulder with a soundless growl and added, "Clumsy oaf!"

Dr. Craven gazed at him, wondering why he disliked his son so much—and wondering how awkward, how dangerous that dislike might soon prove.

Dr. Bedlo defiantly returned the gaze for as long as he could; then, averting his eyes, he sank back on his seat and proceeded to mope for a while.

The coach had come onto the main road, which skirted the edge of a steep cliff. Far below, the surf crashed whitely on dark and jagged rocks. Its sound mingled with, and every so often was covered by, the ominous rumbles of a nearing storm.

And now the coach was rounding a cliffside curve. Dr. Bedlo looked out of his window, then at Dr. Craven, who was sitting opposite him. "I don't understand this slighting attitude you have toward magic," the fat little sorcerer said. If I possessed the power I saw you demonstrate before—I wouldn't be so casual about it.

"And yet," Dr. Craven told him, "*I* despise to use that power, sir."

"Then you're a *fool.*"

"Am I?" Dr. Craven thought for a moment. Then he leaned forward, tried to explain. "What *is* magic, sir, but an interference with the normal order of events, a subversion of the natural?" His tone was patient and a trifle pedantic. "Therefore, magic is *un*natural—and not worthy of desire. Except to those who reject and hate what nature has bestowed upon them."

"Perhaps nature has bestowed *less* upon them than on others," Dr. Bedlo countered tightly. "Perhaps they seek to rectify this in the only way remaining."

Dr. Craven could say no more. He nodded sympathetically.

Outside, high on the driver's box, Rexford Bedlo had become sufficiently accustomed to his vehicle the spirited beasts that drew it, and the hazardous road it traveled, to attempt a conversation with his charming companion. He turned to her. "What was that about your coachman before?" he asked.

"Well," Estelle said slowly, as near as we were able to establish—when he went out to the stable to prepare the coach—something—happened to him."

Staring forward—the road was becoming more tortuous, curving more sharply—Estelle was thinking of Grimes as she had seen him standing before the stable, of the wind sounds, so very like those she heard now, of the lightning almost identical to that which now sheared at the darkened sky ahead. She didn't see Rexford. She didn't see the dull red spot that had suddenly appeared in the center of Rexford's forehead. She didn't notice it getting larger and brighter, didn't notice Rexford's face gradually going blank.

"Father said that, obviously, he was the victim of some diabolic mind control," she continued, shuddering at the memory of what she, and only she, had seen. "Whatever it was, the look on his face was—*hideous.* His eyes were glittering like those of a maniac. And he had his lips pulled back—and twisted—and his teeth clenched. His breath was—harsh—and very rapid."

As Estelle had spoken, stared forward, thought, the very things she had described had begun to be true of Rexford. But first, the spot on his forehead had grown and had reached a peak of glowing intensity; it had assumed a strange, crablike form; and then it had disappeared, seemingly burning through his skull as it did. The wind sounds have died now, to be replaced, after an instant of deathly silence, by a low, eerie hissing.

And suddenly, Rexford brought the whip hard over the horses' rumps, and the coach started picking up speed.

Estelle turned toward him. "Don't you think we'd better go a little—" And seeing his face, his expression, which was exactly like that she had seen on Grimes' face, she broke off in shocked silence, shrinking from him, yet keeping her eyes fixed in dumb horror on his profile.

Again he brought down the whip, and again, over and over. And each time, the horses responded quickly, eagerly. And the coach was moved faster—faster.

"Father?" Estelle whispered, reacting at last. Then she shouted, "*Father!*" And she started to look back, toward the inside of the coach.

But now Rexford had grabbed her around the neck. Now he had his hand covering her mouth, and he was pulling her about, bringing her close to him, close to his distorted face.

She struggled against him, unable to cry out, unable to break his powerful grip.

And then, as she struggled only fitfully, Rexford grinned insanely at her, shrieking the while to the horses, urging them to go faster—faster.

The two passengers inside the coach were rocking on their seats, being thrown forward, then back, bounced to one side, then to the other.

"*Now* what does that idiot think he's doing?" Dr. Bedlo asked irritably. He tried to look over his shoulder and snarl in Rexford's direction, but he couldn't quite manage it. He snarled anyway. Then, clutching the handloop to his right, he opened the window and leaned out, squinted upward, and bellowed, "What's the matter with you?"

For answer, he heard only an eerie hissing, felt only the blast of wind caused by the speeding coach itself.

"I'm *talking* to you Rexford!" he shouted.

And now Rexford turned and smiled down at him, tautly, twistedly, hideously.

Quickly, Dr. Bedlo pulled his head back into the coach. There was a moment when he was too stunned to do anything. Then, shutting the window, he whined, *"He looks exactly like your coachman did!"*

"What!" Dr. Craven gasped. He lunged for the window on his right, opened it, and leaning out, looked toward the driver's box—to see Rexford gripping Estelle with his right hand, gripping the reins with his left. He heard Rexford's shrilled commands to the horses, and he knew from the motion of the coach, from the coarsening of the wind in his face, that the horses were obeying—the horses were going faster.

He looked down now. And gasping again, he realized that the coach was far over on the road, racing along the very edge of the cliff. At the next curve—sooner perhaps—it would plunge over, drop terrifyingly, then crash and splinter on the surf-foamed rocks below.

Pulling his head back inside, Dr. Craven closed the window, then pressed into the corner of the coach, staring dazedly at the man opposite him.

"Well," Dr. Bedlo asked, "why don't you do what you did before?"

"And leave the coach without a driver?"

Now it was Dr. Bedlo who gasped. He hadn't thought of this.

Outside, Rexford was still holding Estelle, still shouting fiercely to the horses, urging them to greater speed, urging them toward the fatal curve. And now that curve was but a dozen lengths ahead. Eight lengths. Six.

All of a sudden Rexford's forehead was glowing, and something crablike, very red, and very bright, seemed to be crawling on it, moving very quickly, twisted outward through the skin. Then, within the instant, it was gone—vanished as if some powerful hand had reached down, ripped it away, and crushed it to nothingness. And in that same instant, a hissing noise became a growl of far-off thunder, and Rexford's features slackened abruptly, leaving his face a total blank.

Estelle was slumped against Rexford, trapped by his rigid arm. The horses were galloping wildly along the edge of the cliff. And four lengths ahead was the curve.

Two lengths now. But now Rexford had released Estelle, who was falling away from him. He was glancing at her in fearful apology, about to reach out and stay her fall.

One length. He reached for the reins instead, pulling in with all his might, shouting, "Whoa! Whoa! *Whoa!*"

The coach jerked violently backward, then forward again onto the start of the curve, only a hairsbreadth from the precipice.

And Rexford held the horses, held them tight, their forelegs pawing the air as they fought against him, fought for their freedom, fought to complete their doom.

Estelle had recovered from her fall. She seized at the reins, putting her hands just below Rexford's. And she, too, pulled back, helping Rexford, fighting the horses, using all of her strength, and at the same time, praying—panting and gasping and praying for more.

Time seemed to be suspended. Seconds were minutes; minutes, hours. The horses relaxed a little. They pawed less savagely, with diminished speed, with diminished force—and finally, not at all. Estelle let go of the reins, mumbled a fervent prayer of thanks. And very slowly, very carefully, Rexford let the horses down. The coach was safe. The travelers were safe.

Rexford turned to Estelle in concern. "Did I hurt you?" he asked.

Her lips formed a silent, "No." Then she smiled at him and patted his hand in sympathy.

Dr. Bedlo and Dr. Craven were still sitting in more or less the same positions they had been thrown to when the coach stopped short. But they were sitting weakly now, staring at each other in glassy-eyed silence.

After several moments, Dr. Bedlo started to say something. But Dr. Craven had already opened the door and was already climbing down from the coach. A few moments later, Dr. Bedlo heard the sound of his and Rexford's voices, but through he listened intently, he could not hear what was being said.

The voices stopped. Then Rexford's face appeared at the door, and shutting the door after him, Rexford got in and settled himself on the seat that had been Dr. Craven's. "He decided that it might be safer for him to drive," Rexford said sheepishly.

Dr. Bedlo glowered at him. The coach began again to move.

"It wasn't *my* fault, Father."

Dr. Bedlo was too exhausted to do anything more than glower. He did, however, manage to glower a little harder.

"It was Dr. Scarabus' doing," Rexford said, trying to make peace.

"Would you kindly shut your mouth?" This was a question. Dr. Bedlo asked it, and in the asking, used up all that remained of his depleted energies.

Not until the coach was nearing Dr. Scarabus' castle did Adolphus Bedlo speak again. And even then, it was only to mutter glumly, "Nothing ever works out right. It's the story of my life."

Rexford Bedlo stayed prudently silent.

Soon the coach was slowing, crossing the narrow bridge that connected the road with the rocky promontory on which Dr. Scarabus' castle stood. From their separate windows, the two Bedlos gazed mutely at the bleak and foreboding structure that they were approaching—that they had stopped before.

Rexford was the first to leave the coach. Adolphus graciously allowed the boy to help him down. Then, when Dr. Craven and Estelle had alighted from the box and were standing beside him and Rexford, he tugged at Dr. Craven's arm and whispered to him, "Don't you think that you and I should go in alone?"

"To what avail, sir?" Dr. Craven shrugged. "Obviously, Scarabus' magic is not confined to the walls of his castle."

Turning then, Dr. Craven led the way to the door of that castle. Estelle was next to him, with Rexford close behind. And in the faltering rear was Adolphus Bedlo, wringing his hands and looking very worried indeed.

Suddenly, the first three stopped in their tracks, and the laggard scampered up to join them. All had heard the sharp click of bolts rapidly withdrawn on the other side of the door. And now they heard the grating of hinges and they saw the door slowly but continuously inching back, then, when it was halfway open, shuddering slightly and coming to a halt.

They stared at the door in confusion. They stared into the darkness beyond it. Then they stared at one another.

At last, Rexford started forward, crossed over the threshold, disappeared for seemingly endless moments.

The others—Dr. Craven, Estelle, and Dr. Bedlo, who had surreptitiously stepped a few paces back, and after those, a few more to bring him well and truly into the best position from which to initiate a retreat—waited silently, fearfully,

Rexford reappeared. He stood in the doorway, and he announced in an ominous voice, *"There's no one here."* Then he went back into the castle.

Chapter 8

DR. CRAVEN smiled reassuringly at his daughter. Then, giving her his hand—and no time to think—he led her through the half open door.

Dr. Bedlo, tense and dubious, toddled along in their wake.

Now the four excursionists stood together in the vast gloom of Dr. Scarabus' entry hall. They saw no one. And they heard nothing but the sounds of their own fear-quickened breathing.

The hall, which was pentagonal in shape and some two stories high, had clearly been conceived and decorated by someone dedicated to the occult—in its blackest aspects. Bizarre paintings and tapestries hung on the ebony-paneled walls. Grotesque statuary stood in seemingly total disorder all about the tilted floor and also here and there on the steps of the great flight that spiraled up to the floor above. The furniture was dark hued, massive, heavily and oddly carved. The draperies, what few there were, and the upholstery were all made of the same leaden velvet into which had been cut a variety of ancient and evil mystic devices.

Although two enormous multibranched iron chandeliers depended from the lofty ceiling, the hall was unlighted save for a pair of black tapers in a curiously wrought wall sconce just to the left of the door. For many moments, the visitors—surely they were interlopers—remained near this, surveying the hall and peering warily into its shadows. Then, suddenly, before Rexford could catch it, the door slammed shut.

Rexford tried to open it, but he couldn't. Shouldering him away,

Dr. Bedlo tried also, also failed. Panicking slightly as he gripped at and continued to pull the large snake-shaped bar that was the door's handle, he turned to Dr. Craven, said in a low hiss, "*You* open it."

"I have not come all this way to flinch at a locked door," Dr. Craven declared. Then, taking a step forward, he called out, "Dr. Scarabus!"

He waited, but was answered only by the distant echo and re-echo of his own voice.

"Dr. *Scarabus!*" he called again, louder.

And the echoes thickened and returned in a futile and eerie counterpoint.

Twitching sharply, Dr. Bedlo had given up trying to open the door to clutch at Dr. Craven's arm. But Dr. Craven had already decided that calling out was useless. Taking the hapless, stumbling Bedlo with him, he moved farther into the hall, Estelle and Rexford followed.

They walked slowly, their footsteps clicking on the tiles and re-sounding now from in front, now from behind, now to one side, now to the other in the vast silence that was everywhere about.

Suddenly, Rexford and Estelle stopped. And turning back to discover why, Drs. Craven and Bedlo saw that Rexford was pointing to a thread of flickering firelight that showed beneath double doors far to the right. Leading the others across the hall, Rexford braced himself, then, very quickly, pushed these doors inward.

A cheery blaze was crackling in the huge fireplace at the end of the room, which was plainly the dining hall of the castle—and even more plainly, untenanted. The four visitors stepped inside. Then, gasping almost as one, they stopped.

In the room's center was a great table laden with food and wine. A place had been set at its head. And two places had been set at each side. In all, five places waited for occupants who—to judge from the table's general condition, the freshness of the food, the steam that rose from many of the platters—were expected momentarily.

"I'm afraid, Father," Estelle said uneasily, and started to turn for the doors. "Hadn't we better—?" Gasping again she broke off and staggered back against the table, shocked.

The others whirled around.

Looking at them from just inside the open doors was Dr. Scarabus, a tall man, elderly but erect, dressed in a long black robe and wearing a black skullcap on his balding and disproportionately large head. "*Afraid,* my child?" he asked, gesturing toward Estelle and smiling genially to allay her concern. "But there is nothing to fear. I welcome you—one and all."

Estelle remained silent, as did Dr. Craven, and the Bedlos.

And now Dr. Scarabus approached them, smiling still and holding out his hand. "You are Dr. Craven, are you not?" Without waiting for an answer, he reached for and gripped Dr. Craven's hand; then, squeezing it in both of his, he went on, "How pleased I am to meet you after all these years. The son of Roderick Craven in my home at last. Your father and I were old comrades, you know."

"*Comrades?*" Dr. Craven repeated, surprised.

But Dr. Scarabus had already dropped his hand to turn to Estelle. "And who is this lovely child?" Cutting off Dr. Craven's reply, he gazed at Estelle, who tried to smile, but managed only to cringe a little farther back against the table.

"No," Dr. Scarabus said, ignoring this by looking again at Dr. Craven, "no, tell me nothing!" He turned back to Estelle, peered at her. "Ah, yes, the lineage is clear. Your *daughter.* Estelle is it not? Thrice welcome to the home of Dr. Scarabus, my dear. How enchanting you are."

And as she nodded, cringed, sought to murmur something polite, he turned once more, this time to point suddenly at Rexford. "And *this* fine fellow?" He looked at Dr. Craven. "Surely not your *son,* dear doctor?"

"I am Dr. Bedlo's son," Rexford said calmly.

"Of course!" Dr. Scarabus exclaimed. Then, nodding and smiling at Dr. Bedlo, he said, "The resemblance is uncanny."

Dr. Bedlo was fully cognizant of the contrast between the handsome boy and his fat and ugly self. He stiffened gloweringly. But before he could say a word, Dr. Scarabus had turned back to Dr. Craven and was rambling on. "But what happy circumstances brings you here, dear Dr. Craven?"

"The spirit of my late wife, sir," Erasmus Craven answered gravely.

"Spirit, doctor?" The elderly necromancer made his face a blank. "Late wife?" He shook his head. "I'm afraid I do not understand you."

"Dr. Bedlo has informed me," Erasmus Craven interrupted what would have been a continuing stream of protests, "that he saw my wife—Lenore—within these walls." He waited a moment, challenging the old man. "Is it true sir? Have you her soul in bondage?"

"*Dr. Craven.*" Dr. Scarabus was aghast, or at least, apparently so. "I am *shocked*, sir. Shocked that you could entertain such an appalling thought. Do you really believe that I would, willingly, commit such a heinous outrage upon the soul of a departed human being? Oh, *sir*. You would wound me to the heart." He held his hand over his chest and shook his head again, sorrowfully now. "My life has very nearly reached its end. I am an old and weary man who desires no more than to complete his allotted span in peace and quiet. That you should think me capable of actions so despicable—" Shaking his head, he started to look away, as if his eyes might contain tears.

But Dr. Craven would not allow this. "If it is not true," he demanded, "then why did you try to prevent out arrival?"

"I did *not* try to prevent it, sir."

"But—?"

His expression half indignant, half lugubrious, Dr. Scarabus strode to the bell cord and pulled it twice.

"What are you doing?" Adolphus Bedlo asked, suspicious.

"Summoning forth the truth," Dr. Scarabus replied somberly.

For a moment or so, no more was said. Everyone waited, and turning toward the doors at the sound of footsteps clicking across the entry hall, waited a little longer. Then everyone gasped.

Standing in the shadows of the doorway was a servant girl. Slender and well proportioned, black haired, pale skinned, she looked, at first glance, very much like Lenore. But when she stepped into the light, the resemblance faded immediately. "You rang, sir?" she said. Her voice was that of a peasant.

Dr. Scarabus gestured toward her. "Here is your spirit, Dr. Craven."

Dr. Craven gazed intently at the girl—she was just a servant wench, fetching, but coarse, not at all like Lenore. Then suddenly, he glared at Bedlo, who winced, swallowed hard, and wringing his plump hands, said defensively, "Well—she does look like your wife." He glanced at the girl then back at Dr. Craven. *"Doesn't* she?"

Dr. Craven glared at the little man a moment more. Then, with a grimace of pain, he turned away and walked to the fireplace, where he stood hunched with grief, staring emptily into the flames, and whispering over and over the name of Lenore—his beloved Lenore, his dead Lenore.

Pausing only long enough to give the unfortunate Bedlo a scathing look, Estelle Craven followed her father, and standing beside him, gently touched his arm.

He tried to smile at her, but he couldn't. His eyes were moist, his lips quivering spasmodically. Indeed, very soon now, his whole body would begin to tremble.

Estelle moved from him. She could not bear to see him so shaken, so weak, so submissive to the sorrow he should long ago have overcome. She looked at Dr. Scarabus, and although her own eyes had now blurred with tears, she saw him grinning—evilly, she thought, and delightedly—as, with a casual wave, he dismissed the servant girl from the room.

Once more, the girl's footsteps clicked across the entry hall. And now she was gone.

Estelle was looking at Dr. Scarabus, wondering about him.

Rexford Bedlo was looking, glaring rather, at his father.

And Dr. Adolphus Bedlo, who had lurched to a chair and them assumed a stiff posture on its very edge, was glaring back at his son, curling and uncurling his upper lip as he did.

Suddenly, Dr. Craven turned. He had somewhat recovered himself. He looked toward Dr. Scarabus, said with effort, "My apologies, doctor—for having wronged you." Then he turned back to the flames.

Chapter 9

"WHAT CAN I say to express my sorrow at this gross misunderstanding?" Dr. Scarabus asked in a soft and cooing voice—which quite belied the hurrying steps he was taking toward the fireplace.

"Please, sir"—he stood beside Erasmus Craven and put an imploring hand on his shoulder—"join me at the table. Share a little food and wine and conversation. Let us not part on such a somber note."

Dr. Craven looked up. But he did not look directly at Scarabus; he did not see the hardness, the iron cunning, that sent the reflected firelight glinting too sharply from Scarabus' eyes.

"Would you," Dr. Scarabus continued, "could you make that gesture for an old man's sake?"

"Of course," Erasmus Craven whispered, touched.

"*Thank* you, Dr. Craven. My appreciation is unbounded." Smiling appropriately, he gestured toward the table, gestured again for Estelle, who returned to her father's side, glanced hesitantly at him, then took his arm so that he could escort her.

"Doctor?" The genial host bowed deep to Adolphus Bedlo. Then to Rexford. "Young sir?"

Dr. Bedlo rose. He sneered once more at Rexford. Then he sneered, just once, at Dr. Scarabus covertly, however, and at a moment when the bowing sorcerer couldn't possibly see him. After which, he, and Rexford also, went to the table.

Dr. Scarabus—the kindly old gentleman, hospitable, forgiving, wanting no more than to live out his final years in peace—stood at the table's head, smiling, beaming even, at the son of his departed friend, his treasured friend. "On my right, dear doctor, if you please; your lovely daughter next to you."

Dr. Craven, not quite convinced, and Estelle, thoroughly unconvinced, took the places indicated.

"You at my left, Dr. Bedlo," the host was saying. "And you, young sir." He motioned to the remaining chair.

As he was sitting, Dr. Bedlo glowered, but with his face averted from Dr. Scarabus. Then, growing suddenly bold in spirit, and red of face, he muttered under his breath, "Don't think I've forgotten what happened earlier this evening."

Rexford looked at the senior Bedlo in surprise.

"Ah," Dr. Scarabus said regretfully, "but I had hoped that you *had* forgotten sir."

"Being turned into *raven?*" Dr. Bedlo whined tensely.

"A *raven?*" Rexford asked. He was more than surprised now. Indeed, he was stunned, as was Estelle, who gazed questioningly, first at Dr. Bedlo, then at Dr. Scarabus, and finally, at her father.

"But sir," Dr. Scarabus reminded his accuser in a mild and infinitely patient tone, "you tried to kill me. Under the circumstances, I feel that I acted with extreme leniency. I knew that, presently, you would discover a method by which to restore yourself. And, lo! You have—and all is well again."

"And you didn't try to stop us from coming here, hanh?" Dr. Bedlo was both dubious and scornful.

Dr. Scarabus beamed at him for a moment, then said,

"Have I not convinced you of my sincerity? Why should I try to stop you? Good company is hard to come by"—he paused to glance around the table benignly, and just a bit smugly—"and this is the very *best* of company." And now he held out his hands to his guests and proclaimed with beneficent fervor, "*Please* eat! Drink! Let us enjoy an hour of more pleasant conviviality.

Everyone hesitated, looking uneasily at the food and wine. Then, after grinning at each of his guests in turn, Dr. Scarabus tasted a morsel from every platter of food—as if to demonstrate its harmlessness. And with every bite, he sipped at his wine—showing that it, too, could give no offense.

Dr. Bedlo at least was wholly satisfied. He partook of the wine, and only of the wine. But he drank heavily, lapsing the while deeper and deeper into a brooding and fretful silence.

The other three guests helped themselves to both food and drink, but with extreme moderation.

Wisely, Dr. Scarabus refrained from proposing any toasts.

Dr. Craven was grateful for this, but he was still not quite convinced of his host's sincerity. He turned to him, watching him closely for a moment. Then he said, "You referred to my father as a comrade before, Dr. Scarabus."

"And that he was, sir. The nearest and dearest of comrades."

"I'm sorry," Dr. Craven said awkwardly, "but my father never gave me the impression that you and he were anything but mortal enemies."

"The fiery blood of youth, sir." Dr. Scarabus shrugged then smiled deprecatingly. "The sporadic clash of varying temperaments. We were competitors, yes—contestants, if you will. But enemies? Ah, *no,* dear doctor. The apparent animosity between us was not a deeply rooted as you may have thought. Actually there was a bond of understanding between us. I admired him as I admired no other man. And—I truly hope—that admiration was reciprocated."

"I—see," Dr. Craven said, totally confused now. "And yet—it always appeared—"

Dr. Scarabus raised a gently admonishing finger. "*Ah,*" he said. "*appeared,* dear doctor. We of the occult dedication know but too well the deceptiveness of what appears to be."

"True," Dr. Craven said uncertainly. It was his habit to believe the best of people. He wanted to believe the best of Dr. Scarabus. He smiled at him. "Quite—true," he said, and now he was convinced, or at least, virtually so.

Sensing his victory, Dr. Scarabus smiled back. It was a smile that reassured Dr. Craven. Estelle, however, shuddered instinctively to see it.

"But tell me something of your wonderous hand manipulations, doctor," the elder sorcerer went on. "I have heard miraculous reports about them, and yet I have never witnessed any."

"But I understand that you, too, possess the gift of magic by gesture," Dr. Craven said, puzzled slightly.

"Oh? Who told you that?"

"Dr. Bedlo here." Dr. Craven nodded toward his fellow guest, who was busily downing the contents of his wineglass—an act that would allow him to refill it at the earliest possible moment.

Dr. Scarabus looked at Bedlo with a smile. "I fear that he exaggerated somewhat."

"*Did* I?" Dr. Bedlo asked, and snarled drunkenly.

But Dr. Scarabus had already turned back to the guest of honor. "I am certain," he was saying, "that I am—to no degree—as proficient as yourself. True, I have my humble means, but—"

"*Humble,* anh?" Dr. Bedlo interrupted savagely. Like turning people into *birds?*"

Dr. Scarabus sighed. "I wish you would forget that, sir. The incident is closed."

"*Not to me it isn't.*" Dr. Bedlo leaned toward him, eager to do combat. "Where is my bag of magical equipment?"

"In a safe place, doctor."

"Give it back to me."

"Gladly, doctor. If I may only have your promise not to—"

Suddenly, Dr. Bedlo smashed over his goblet of wine. "I promise nothing!" he shouted. "I only challenge you!"

"Again, sir?" Dr. Scarabus asked, pained.

And Dr. Craven, reaching across the table in an attempt to mediate, said softly, "Dr. Bedlo—"

"Oh, shut your mouth!" Dr. Bedlo cut him off. Then, as Dr. Craven—and Rexford and Estelle—gasped in shock, he turned once more to their host, threw back his shoulders in what was meant to be a show of aggressive strength, and asked, "Are you afraid to face me when I'm sober?"

"*Are* you sober, doctor?" the prospective opponent asked, with a smile that suggested the only possible answer.

And now Dr. Bedlo reared up, letting his chair topple backward, then kicking it out of his way. He stood over Dr. Scarabus and tried to glare at him, but he couldn't quite focus his eyes. He could, however, pound the table. And this he did while, at the same time, he declared thickly. "I'm sober enough to make a fool of you, you old blackguard!"

"Dr. Bedlo!" Erasmus Craven exclaimed.

"Father!" Rexford Bedlo said simultaneously.

Dr. Scarabus had stiffened in his chair, and his face had suddenly gone blank. Now, with great effort, he regained his smile and his air of affability. "I shall pretend," he said slowly, equably, "that you have not spoken, Dr. Bedlo. We will continue with our pleasant little"

Dr. Bedlo began again to pound the table. "You *are* afraid of me, you *miserable coward!*"

"Father!" Rexford Bedlo hissed at him, then caught at and held his hand. "In the name of—!"

"Shut your mouth!" Adolphus Bedlo shouted, drowning him out. Then, pulling loose his hand, he turned back to Dr. Scarabus. And giving the table a final, a mighty, and—he hoped—a definitive thump, he said, *"Aren't* you afraid of me, you ancient hellhound? Afraid to face me in an *honest duel* of magic. He waited a moment, swaggering suddenly. Then, having come around to Dr. Scarabus' other side, he leaned very close to him and whispered, almost in his ear, "Pitiful old goat."

Dr. Scarabus shut his eyes. "Enough," he said tightly.

But Bedlo continued. "Stupid, shriveled-up old—"

"Enough, sir! Dr. Scarabus said, opening his eyes to looked fixedly at Bedlo, and after a moment, to look at Dr. Craven in mute apology.

Dr. Craven smiled sympathetically.

"What am I to do, dear doctor?" his host asked, shrugging as if in defeat.

Dr. Bedlo was still bent over, still leaning close. "Can't you decide for yourself?" he whispered viciously.

And shrugging again, Dr. Scarabus looked again at Bedlo. Then, with a deep sigh, he rose from his place at the head of the table and moved across the room to a large oak cabinet. It jangled slightly as he carried it back to the table, and it clanked loudly as he set it down in front of Dr. Bedlo.

"Aha!" Dr. Bedlo exclaimed, circling the bag with his arms, then clutching it to his puffed-out chest.

"Proceed, sir," Dr. Scarabus said, nodding sorrowfully at him.

"Now!" Adolphus Bedlo's tone was ghoulish. "Now we shall see

who is the master of magicians."

"Sir," Dr. Craven said, "I implore you—"

"Implore me not"—Adolphus Bedlo turned to him and snarled—*"dear doctor."*

Then, straightening as best he could, he wheeled about, and in a series of erratic strides, betook himself and his jangling bag to a small table set between a pair of windows on the other side of the room. A brass urn occupied the center of the table. But Dr. Bedlo was not to be daunted; he slapped at the urn, smiling triumphantly as it bounced on the rug, then rolled from his sight. The table was now clear. He put down his bag and proceeded, busily and clumsily, to undo the straps with which it was fastened.

The others watched him, Rexford Bedlo turning in his chair to do so, and Dr. Scarabus holding onto the back of Dr. Craven's chair. After a moment, Dr. Scarabus went again to the head of the table and sat down again, heavily. And Rexford, with a grimace of concern, stood up, smiled timidly at the worried Estelle, then went across the room to try to dissuade his father.

Dr. Bedlo started slightly as Rexford came up behind him. Then he tangled the thong on which he was working. He swore at the thong, and he swore at the boy. But he kept his eyes, and almost all of his attention, fixed on the former.

"You mustn't do this, Father," Rexford said softly.

Adolphus Bedlo clenched his teeth, and still without turning, without facing Rexford, without so much as glancing at him, he hissed, "Who are you to tell me what not to do? Go back to the table."

"Father," Rexford pleaded, "you're in no condition to—"

"Go away," Adolphus Bedlo interrupted. His tone was one of warning.

"What if he turns you into a raven again.

And now Dr. Bedlo grabbed Rexford by the arm and hurled him toward the table. "I said go away! he snarled as Rexford stood some paces distant and looked at him with a hurt expression.

Dr. Bedlo returned to his tangled thong, managing at last to straighten and disengage it, and then, finally, to pull open his bag.

Rexford, sighing defeatedly, started back to the table.

Dr. Craven, sighing also, glanced unhappily from one to the

other Bedlo. Then, looking at Dr. Scarabus, he asked, "Is there no way to stop this?"

"I have done what I can, sir," Dr. Scarabus said. "But as you can see, he seems intent upon revenge."

After several moments of rummaging in his bag, Dr. Adolphus Bedlo, watched by the three people who were now seated at the table, as well as by Rexford, who was no standing near it, had taken out a device similar in appearance to a miniature wind vane. Setting this down, he had tinkered with it for a few seconds. And then, glowering steadily—both for his own benefit and for that of his audience—he had fished in the bag twice more, coming up first with a black wand, which he set beside his little machine and after that, with a scrap of brightly colored cloth crumpled into a sort of ball.

The ball of cloth he now held aloft, and with a grand flourish, tossed high into the air—where it popped open to become a sorcerer's peaked hat. Holding out his two hands, he waited for it to float down to him. It came lazily. He waited patiently. Even so, he was not quite sober enough to catch it without an ungainly lurch.

Wincing in embarrassment, Rexford Bedlo resumed his place at the table.

Sr. Scarabus lowered his eyes, repressing a smile of amusement.

Dr. Craven looked pained on Bedlo's behalf.

Alone among the company, Estelle Craven continued to look worried.

And now Dr. Bedlo put the hat on his head. The effect was far from impressive. Indeed, did he but know it, the plump little sorcerer looked ridiculous. *"Now,"* he said in a slow and presumably ominous voice, rubbing his hands together and goggling in a fashion calculated—by him—to be awesome and menacing.

Rexford Bedlo groaned. Then, turning from the sight he leaned his elbows on the table and pressed his face into his cupped hands. Estelle regarded him compassionately for a moment. Then, after looking hopefully at her father, who didn't move, and dubiously at Dr. Scarabus, motionless also, she returned her gaze to the senior Bedlo.

"Now," he repeated, still rubbing his hands together, still goggling. Whereupon he set his bag of equipment on the floor and shoved the small table, complete with the vanelike device at its center, to a

position in front of the window to his right. Then, after a short pause to huff back his breath, he picked up his want, and leaning forward, tried to touch it to the device on the table. His approach was similar to that of a man with eye trouble trying to thread a needle. Nevertheless, he kept trying, blinking, shaking is head, and trying again.

Dr. Craven had turned to Bedlo's intended victim. "Be easy on him, doctor," he said.

"I will do what I *can*, sir," Dr. Scarabus answered testily.

After some ten or twenty tries—or more exactly, stabs—at the peculiar little apparatus, Dr. Bedlo rested a moment. Then, gripping his want with both hands, he bent over, and carefully, very carefully, brought it down on top of the device, which began at once to spin. It moved slowly at first, and it creaked a bit. Soon, however, it gained speed, and in doing so, started to hum shrilly and to throw off multicolored sparks.

Straightening, Dr. Bedlo faced the supper table and his audience, which had been reduced by one with the defection of Rexford, who was still hiding his eyes, still unable to look; it consisted now of three persons. Dr. Bedlo glowered at each in turn. Then, with a smile of impending triumph on his drink-slackened features, he raised his want and pointed it clumsily at Dr. Scarabus.

Outside, there was a faint rumbling of thunder.

Dr. Bedlo held to his wand, staggering slightly, but keeping it raised and pointed more or less accurately in the direction of Dr. Scarabus.

And the thunder sounded again, somewhat louder this time.

Now Rexford Bedlo lowered his hands and twisted around in his chair to see what was happening.

Dr. Scarabus, sitting motionless, smiled, louder yet. And now a wind began to rise, howling. And raindrops began to spatter, then to pound against the tall windows.

Dr. Bedlo grinned crookedly. His breath quickened as dropping the wand to his side for a moment, he turned about, first to inspect his humming and spinning and sparkling magical machine, then to peer out of the window before which it stood. Seeing how the storm was progressing, he grinned again. "It's going to work," he hissed, delighted.

Then, turning back toward the supper table, he again raised and pointed the wand at Dr. Scarabus. "It's going to work, you old devil, you!" he shouted, joggling with demoniacal glee. "Now we shall see!" And now the foolish hat tottered on his head, and the want wagged and swooped and circled in his hand as he fairly bounced up and down—waiting.

A streak of lightning raked blue-white across the blackened sky. Then an explosion of thunder deemed to rock the very walls of the castle. The wind shrieked insanely, and the rain throbbed to the ground and cracked against the windows in a constantly accelerating tempo.

Dr. Bedlo tensed and stood still, looking over his shoulder at the storm. Lightning flashed again—closer. The explosion of thunder that followed it was louder and more violent and its reverberations grumbled longer behind the sound of the shrieking wind. Dr. Bedlo's face distorted with excitement. His skin was bleached to whiteness by the continuing lightning.

Dr. Craven looked upward, confused, and at last, worried. Estelle had the back of her left hand pressed to her lips. Gasping, she clenched it and bit on her knuckles, hard. Dr. Craven glanced at her. Then, even as he returned his eyes to Adolphus Bedlo, the window, and the storm, he reached for Estelle's hand, and pulling it from her lips, brought it down to the table, where he straightened it and held it stiffly in his.

Rexford Bedlo remained twisted about in his chair, but he was string now, wide eyed, anxious, and intent.

And Dr. Scarabus sat back, watching, but apparently relaxed. He was still smiling impassively. And his hands were still hidden in his lap.

The storm grew wilder yet—and wilder. The wind was more shrill; the rain fell harder, faster. The lightning was brighter and pitched ever nearer to the castle. The explosions of thunder were more turbulent and reverberated more savagely.

Suddenly, in a great frenzy of exhilaration, Dr. Bedlo raised his arms on high. *"Now we shall see!"* he shouted. *"Now!"*

In the next instant, a streak of lightning crashed through the window, and Adolphus Bedlo disappeared in a soaring burst of flame.

Light flared over the dining hall, over the table, and over those who were seated around it. Estelle Craven was screaming, sobbing, screaming again. Her father's hand was clamped on hers. He, and Rexford Bedlo also, were immobile, seemingly incapable of motion. Dr. Scarabus had removed his hands from his lap and was using them to cover his mouth. He was chuckling—hysterically perhaps—or perhaps at some private joke.

In a moment, the light was gone, leaving only the wind, softer now, and the rain, slower and a little erratic, and a distant rumble of thunder. Estelle had stopped screaming, and her sobs were stifled and weak. She, and the others, sat woodenly, looking toward the window.

Then they looked up, watching Dr. Bedlo's peaked hat as it floated gracefully to the floor.

Chapter 10

DR. CRAVEN moved first. Standing shakily, he pushed back his chair, left the table, and walked across the room to the spot where Bedlo had been. When he reached it, he looked down. Only a gust of wind and a splattering of icy rain that pelted against his forehead through the shattered window kept him from being sick—or so at least he thought.

On the floor was a dark puddle, brownish-red in color, glutinous in consistency, and of no shape whatsoever. Portions of it bubbled slightly, exuding a pale yellow smoke that carried with it the faint but unmistakable bouquet of stale wine. The puddle, the vapor, and nearby, the absurd peaked hat—to all appearances, nothing remained of Adolphus Bedlo.

Dr. Craven leaned forward to get a better view of the puddle. Then, in a kind of stupor, he bent, reached down, and dipped his finer into it. Raising the finger, he gaped at the blob of brownish-red stuff that was sticking to it. "Oh, dear," he mumbled dully.

As Dr. Craven was trying to wipe his finger clean of the elder Bedlo—rubbing it with a handkerchief, rubbing it on the rougher cloth of his sleeve—Rexford had struggled to his feet, and with some difficulty, propelled himself across the room.

"That's *him?*" Rexford asked weakly, looking down at the puddle with a bilious grimace.

Dr. Craven had started at the sound of Rexford's voice. Guiltily he hid the soiled finger behind his back. Then he stood erect beside the boy and gazed at him for a moment. But he could find nothing to say. He shook his head slowly, sadly. Then, together, he and Rexford stared at the floor and at the smoking mess that was on it.

A few moments later, Estelle and Dr. Scarabus joined them. Clutching at her father's arm, Estelle averted her face almost immediately. Dr. Scarabus—after he had fastidiously hiked up the hem of his long black robe—proclaimed in a funereal tone, "He should not have tried for that particular effect."

Rexford Bedlo twitched slightly. Then he looked at Dr. Scarabus with an expression that was at once aggrieved, hostile, and tremulous—questioning, and equally, accusing.

The old sorcerer smiled benignly. "It requires such total concentration," he said.

And now Dr. Craven looked up, dazed.

Dr. Scarabus devoted the smile to him. "If I may suggest it," he said, "I think that, perhaps, your daughter should lie down, dear doctor. The shock of all this—"

Estelle's hand tightened on her father's arm. Then, releasing it, she gazed pleadingly at him. "We must leave now, Father," she said, and started toward the doors.

"Leave?" Dr. Scarabus asked, gesturing as if to hold her back. "Ah, but *no,* my dear. The storm is far tooviolent. Stay until the morning—and leave, *refreshed.*"

Estelle had stopped. She was afraid—more afraid as Dr. Scarabus beamed at her, then beamed at her father, coaxing them to remain within his walls.

Lightning flashed outside, and the rain pelted harder. Once again, the storm was beginning to rage.

"Good night, Father," Estelle said, smiling.

Her smile faded as soon as she had shut the door of the room to which Dr. Scarabus had assigned him.

Her own room was farther down the hallway, almost at its end. She walked toward it slowly, hesitating often, glancing nervously now at this shadow, now at that. And she breathed a deep sigh of relief when she had at last traversed the necessary distance and stood, quite safe, before the door of her room.

"Murdered—!" Estelle stepped back, horrified.

Rexford gestured urgently for her to remain calm—and to lower her voice.

She nodded dumbly at him. Then, after a moment, she asked, "Why did you say that?"

"Because, while my father was attempting his magical effect—I observed Dr. Scarabus—hands in lap—*making furtive motions with his fingers.*"

Estelle caught her breath. "Then father was right."

"About what?"

"He just told me a few moments ago that he was confused as to how the means utilized by your father could have summoned forth such a storm."

"They *couldn't* have," Rexford said grimly. "Father was *murdered.*"

"And yet"—Estelle shook her head, trying to understand—"Why now? Scarabus had your father at his mercy earlier this evening and didn't kill him then.

"Perhaps father was not as abusive to him then," Rexford answered. He shrugged puzzledly. Then he looked at Estelle, and touching her arm, said "But we must speak to your father; convince him of the danger we are in."

"I have already spoken to him," Estelle said. "All in vain. He seems to regard Dr. Scarabus as completely worthy of trust."

"Perhaps if I told him what I saw—regarding Dr. Scarabus' hand motions—?"

"That *might* convince him." Estelle smiled, feebly but hopefully.

"We shall have to try," Rexford said, and turning for the door, he started as if to open it. He pulled; pulled harder. The door seemed to be locked. He pulled again. It was locked—from the other side.

Estelle stared at him in alarm.

Sighing again, she opened it and went in. Then, as she closed it behind her and turned, a hand shot out to cover her mouth. The scream that was rising to her lips sounded forth as no more than a faint gasp of terror, smothered nearly to the point of being inaudible.

"*Shhh!*" Rexford Bedlo warned, and when Estelle had somewhat relaxed, and her involuntary struggles had subsided into weak little twitches of anger and surprise, he took away his hand.

She stared at him.

"I'm sorry," he said softly. "I thought that someone might hear."

"What do you want?"

He hesitated a moment before he answered. "Perhaps you wondered why I said nothing tonight when—when my father—" And he broke off, wincing at the painful memory.

"I understand," Estelle murmured sympathetically.

"No," he said. "No, you don't. I said nothing because I did not want Dr. Scarabus to deduce what I was thinking."

"What?"

"That we are all in danger of our lives," he said gravely. "That Scarabus *murdered* my father."

"Already it begins," he said very quietly.

"What are we to do?" Estelle asked, frightened.

Rexford gazed at her for a moment, thinking. Then he turned quickly and moved across the room to the windows, one of which he pushed open. The storm had abated somewhat. But it was still raining; still windy. Every so often, pale lightning streaked the distant sky, or lighted it for a fleeting instant; every so often, there was a growl of far-off thunder.

As Estelle came to Rexford's side, he was leaning over the sill of the window, looking down. She, too, looked down—and gasping, shrank back to avoid the sight of the dark sea crashing on the rocks far below.

"What are you staring at?" she asked Rexford.

Straightening, he pointed downward and to his right. There's a narrow ledge out there."

"You're not going to try to—?"

"I *must* reach your father, Estelle. Only he can get us out of this."

Estelle went to the window again and looked now at the ledge to which Rexford had pointed. Then, shuddering back, she said tightly, earnestly, "But you'll *kill* yourself."

"Better killed like that than helpless and defeated in Scarabus' hands," Rexford said, and giving Estelle no time to argue with him, no time to dissuade him, no time to stay the beat of his courage, he climbed onto the sill, crouched, and let his right leg dangle against the outside wall for a moment.

The wind tore at that leg, and the rain soaked and made heavy the cloth with which it was covered. Gritting his teeth, Rexford

82

stiffened it and swung it as close as he could to the ledge. Then he peered down, and carefully not looking too low—not looking at the sharp rocks or the vicious sea that churned over and around them—he tried to judge the distance he would have to drop.

At last he drew back the leg, turned about on the sill, and pausing only long enough to suck in a deep breath, began to climb downward, hands clutching at the sill, feet slapping against the wall, digging into one of its crevices, slapping out again, digging into a crevice below.

Standing away from the window, Estelle stared in anguish at his hands. She saw them tighten when, having climbed as far as he could, he let himself hang free. She saw the subtle shifting of his wrists as, bracing himself, he forced his body to the right.

And then, with a stifled gasp, she saw his fingers jerk open and apart.

He was falling now—down—down—

Estelle ran to the window, looked toward the ledge. Rexford had landed on it. Rexford was safe. She closed her eyes for a moment, breathing heavily, trying not to cry out.

Then, when she opened them, looked again, she saw that Rexford was not safe. He was losing his footing, staggering, starting to topple backward. She gasped, and in the very instant of her gasp, he caught at a projection on the wall. He was holding it now, pulling himself up, up—pulling himself out of danger.

"Are you all right?" Estelle called softly as soon as she was able to do so.

"All right," he answered panting.

He gazed at Estelle for several moments, and she at him.

Then, taking in a wavering breath, he tore his eyes from her to glance to his either side, find out just where, exactly, all his efforts had brought him.

Estelle saw a look of dismay cross his face before, smiling, he gazed back up at her again. She saw his lips moving. But the wind was too loud now; his words were lost. She tried to smile, but she couldn't.

The wind was lashing at Rexford. The rain was pounding him, and it was making the narrow ledge treacherously slippery. And far below, the sharp rocks waited, and the dark sea boomed, ready to lick him from them.

He had started to move along the ledge, very slowly, very carefully, pressing himself against the wall at every step. For an instant, Estelle thought she saw him lose his balance. But, no. He was merely holding to the wall, hesitating at some obstacle. Soon he had passed it.

Soon afterwards he was so far from Estelle that, lean from the window as she might, she could barely see him. And then she couldn't see him at all.

Erasmus Craven was sitting in front of the fireplace in his bedroom, gazing now at the flames, now at the palm of his right hand, in which he held a tiny oil miniature of Lenore. There were tears in his eyes, and his skin was flushed, possibly from the heat of the fire. After a while he realized that he had begun to tremble.

He slid the miniature into one of his pockets then, and getting to his feet, he paced restlessly up and down the room.

At last, so weary that he could pace no longer, he came to a stop before a set of French doors. These doors, which opened onto a battlement walk, were near the far corner of the room; set into the wall adjoining, the wall to which he had his back, was a bay of latticed windows, and this bay jutted out over the same walk to which the doors gave access. Dr. Craven had noted this earlier. But he was only dimly aware of it now. Now he was trying to concentrate on the storm, to fix all of his attention on its ferocity—to think of nothing else.

Suddenly, he whirled about.

Someone was standing at the farthest window, peering from the darkness of the walk into the lighted room—watching him.

Feverish, apprehensive, he stared at the window. But it was too dark. There was too much rain. He could see only a shadow, the outline of a figure. Yet there was something familiar—something unmistakable—

He lunged toward the window, and in the same instant a flash of lightning allowed him to see the face of—

"Lenore!" He shrieked her name, and arms thrown wide, he staggered toward her. But she was gone.

Erasmus Craven stood dazed and immobile for a moment, looking at the spot from which Lenore had flitted. He was stricken, horrified, desperately confused. His face was distorted with pain. His arms were rigid and still thrown wide.

Then, abruptly, he went limp. And even more abruptly, he stiffened and rushed to the French doors, jerked them open and pitched out onto the storm-swept walk. Hurrying along next to the battlement, staring widely this way, then that, he turned the corner, and an instant later, came to a stop outside the window at which Lenore had stood. But he could find no trace of Lenore.

Lurching forward again, he moved along the walk until he came to a dead end. But, still, he could find no trace of Lenore. Choking back his sobs, he stood trembling and looking toward the heavens, letting the wind tear against him and the rain pelt into his eyes. Then, brokenly, he spoke her name, "Lenore—"

Chapter 11

LENORE CRAVEN removed her rain-sodden cloak and dropped it to the floor, unhooked her wet dress and stepped out of it. She was starting to take off a petticoat when, turning abruptly, she saw that Dr. Scarabus was sitting in a large high-backed chair, smiling dispassionately as he watched her.

She shrugged, and not in the least concerned, continued to undress. "Did you have to make it *rain?*" she asked with just a touch of petulance in her deeply melodious voice.

"You had to see him, didn't you?"

"I was curious." She offered Dr. Scarabus a faint, teasing smile. "I thought I'd take a look at him—as long as he's here."

"*No thanks to you,*" Dr. Scarabus said sharply, and countered her smile with a frown.

Lenore was down now to the bare essentials of underclothing. Going to her dressing table, she stood before the mirror and primped for a moment, then sat and began to unpin her hair.

How was I to know that you *wanted* him here?" she said, taking out the last pin. "You never tell me anything." Her ebony tresses fell loose around her face. She flipped them sensuously, and perhaps a bit sarcastically over one shoulder, then over the other.

Then, picking up a large carved-ivory comb, she held it cocked in the air while she said, pouting slightly, "I was afraid he'd find out about me and cause an unpleasant scene."

"So you decided to have him killed in preference, is that it?"

Dr. Scarabus leaned forward, waiting for her to answer.

She shrugged breezily and began to comb her hair.

Whereupon he got to his feet, and moving behind her, circled her throat with his hands. "And would you have the same thing done to me?" he asked, rubbing his thumbs against the sides of her neck. "To avoid an unpleasant scene?"

Lenore looked at him in the mirror. "Your hands are so dry," she said, and grimaced up at his reflection.

Dr. Scarabus gazed a moment at the image of her beautiful, vain face reflected below his old one. Then, sighing, he released his hands.

Lenore went on combing her hair, arranging it about her shoulders and down her back, primping, while he straightened and moved away, paced for a few moments, then sitting down nearby, began again to watch her.

"Once more I stand in awe and admiration of your utter lack of scruples," he said, smiling thinly.

Absorbed in a particular curl, Lenore answered casually, "You knew what you were getting. Did i ever pretend it was your *charm* that brought me here? She wrapped the curl about her finger, and holding it, leaned forward to study him in the mirror. "I came for your wealth—for your power. And gave you, in return, my—*company.*" The curl sprang loose and snapped into place behind her ear; she patted it there; then she shrugged, said, "If you insist on more, you shall only succeed in boring me—at which point I will leave you as I left Erasmus."

"*How*, my darling treasure?" He smiled again. "By making *me* think that you have died?"

"Hardly. I wouldn't waste my time like that again."

"You never waste your time, do you, my black angel?"

"I wasted enough of it on Erasmus," she said, letting another curl spring from her finger.

"You don't respect him, do you?"

"Res*pect* him?" she said scornfully. "That gullible, ineffectual boor?"

"Gullible—perhaps," Dr. Scarabus answered slowly. "Ineffectual—no." Then, crossing his arms over his chest, he gazed at Lenore with an inscrutable smile.

She continued with her toilet.

And after a moment, he said, "Speaking of him, my precious viper, how did you ascertain that he was coming here? Since, as you pointed out so petulantly—I didn't tell you."

"I didn't know—at first. I only guessed. After you had turned that dismal little fat man into a blackbird—"

"Raven, my dear," Dr. Scarabus interrupted, correcting her.

"Whatever." Lenore shrugged once more. She could not be concerned with such trifles. "Anyway, I knew that he wouldn't *dare* go for help to any magician who was a member of the Brotherhood."

Dr. Scarabus grinned appreciatively. Which left Dr. Craven, of course. How deftly nimble is your mind."

"And," Lenore went on, "Since Bedlo had seen me here, it occurred to me that he might, accidentally, see a painting of me at Erasmus' house—and give it all away. As he *did*, the idiot." Twisting about in her chair now, she looked directly at Dr. Scarabus to ask him in a puzzled tone, "Speaking of *that*, how did *you* know that Bedlo would see a painting of me? If you wanted Erasmus here, wasn't that an awfully farfetched way to go about it?"

"After more than two years with me, *dear* Lenore, do you really think I made my plans in farfetched ways?" He gazed blandly at her. "That I leave anything to chance?"

She sat up straight, put down her comb with a sharp click. "What do you mean by that?"

And rising from his chair, Dr. Scarabus went to her, stood beside her for a moment, then extended his hand to help her up. "Come along, and you shall see," he said softly, and reached down to take the hand she hadn't given him.

Lenore looked at him suspiciously for several moments. Then she allowed him to assist her to her feet.

Rexford Bedlo had come to a corner, and turning it, keeping close, close to the saving wall, he had found that on its other side the ledge was even narrower—scarcely large enough to hold the tentative foot he first placed on it—and its surface was even more slippery. Too, the weather was even harsher, for the storm itself was growing increasingly violent, and Rexford was now more exposed to it, heading directly into the driving rain, directly into the vicious and bitter wind. And more, as if on purpose to add to the discomfort of Rexford's position, if not necessarily to its precariousness, the promontory on which the castle was built dipped sharply on this side, leaving the ledge, and Rexford on it, even higher above the sea, even higher above the deadly spurs of rock that defined its edge.

Rain filled Rexford's eyes, blurring his vision, and at times, depriving him of it entirely. Yet he could not, he dare not, let go of the wall. Half blind, he had no hand with which to wipe away the streaming water that was blinding him.

Worse, he could not look forward. Whenever he tried, gust after gust of wind ripped and clawed at his face—so badly that he had to close his eyes, jam them shut and turn them immediately back to the wall, or to the sea below. He could not tell where he was going, could not tell where, if anywhere, the ledge was taking him.

Nevertheless, he moved on, breathing heavily, sometimes not breathing at all, taking slow, laborious steps, and always, clutching desperately at the wall holding to it for dear life, and hoping—hoping.

And then, soon in fact, but after what seemed like hours, he could go no farther. He was against some sort of a barrier, something that felt like a low railing. Beyond it—?"

He couldn't turn back. For one thing, he was too exhausted to travel again the way he had come. For another, even if he did make it, and he was certain that he couldn't, he would find himself stranded below Estelle's room, unable to climb the distance he had jumped, unable to reach the window and the dubious safety of the locked room beyond it, unable to reach Estelle—who was depending upon him.

He had no choice. He prayed for a moment. And then he released is right hand from the wall, and very quickly, grabbed downward at the barrier.

He had toppled onto a small balcony. He closed his eyes again and passed out from the exhaustion.

When he regained consciousness he discovered that he had to lie for a moment longer on its floor, and oblivious to the scouring of wind and rain across him, he uttered a prayer of thanks. Then he struggled to his feet, and with some difficulty, opened the pair of French doors that connected the balcony to the dark interior of the castle.

He was in a large, and totally unlighted, chamber. Probably a bedroom, he thought. And there might well be someone asleep in it. Drawing in a deep breath, and he hoped a silent one, he started to tiptoe toward the place he thought the hallway door was likeliest to be.

He had gone about halfway across the room and was beginning to breathe a little more easily when suddenly, a figure leaped out of the darkness, and seizing him by the neck, tried simultaneously to choke him and to wrench him backwards to the floor.

Rexford was taller than his assailant—considerably taller. And he was stronger. Even now he was stronger.

He tore the man's fingers from around his throat, whirled as the other lunged, and after a few moments of violent battle, managed to get hold of the man's wildly flailing right arm. Twisting it, he forced the man to his knees. Then, letting it go, he shoved and slapped him to the floor, dropped on top of him, and started to pummel him with his fists.

He was just beginning to unleash some of his heavier blows— when a sudden flash of lightning caused him to pull back, and gagging in shock, to gape down at Adolphus Bedlo, who was glaring up at him in a fury.

"Stop that, you idiot!" Dr. Bedlo hissed softly, but nonetheless fiercely.

Rexford jerked his hands to his sides.

"And now," Dr. Bedlo said, "will you kindly get off my chest?"

Rexford shut his mouth with a gasp. He blinked his staring eyes. And as Dr. Bedlo began to growl menacingly at him, he literally sprang to his feet, but only to gape at Dr. Bedlo again, to look at him in dumb confusion.

Meanwhile, Dr. Bedlo was trying to stand up. He had, after numerous clumsy attempts, succeeded in getting himself into a sitting posture. But this, to all appearances, was as far as he was going to go. He glowered at Rexford, and quivering with rage, hissed up at him, "Why don't you do something to *help* me?"

Gulping nervously, Rexford obeyed. But as soon as Dr. Bedlo was standing, and even before he had dropped Dr. Bedlo's hand, he relapsed into wide-eyed, wide-mouthed staring, and with it, puzzled, spasmodic shaking of his head.

"Stop looking at me as if I were a ghost," the elder Bedlo said sourly.

"But I saw you killed!" Rexford said, almost shouting at him.

"Shhh!" Dr. Bedlo held up a warning finger. "*Softly*. I only wanted Scarabus to *think* that I was dead—so that I'd be free to act in case he moved against the rest of you."

"He already has."

"*What?*" Dr. Bedlo asked, stiffening.

"I just now almost killed myself coming here from Miss Craven's room. She's locked in."

"What were you doing in *her* room? Dr. Bedlo asked, his tone that of a suspicious father.

Rexford looked at him in surprise. "Father, that's beside the point." He looked at him a moment longer, stepped a few paces back, and gestured urgently, pleadingly. "I was warning her if you must know. The point is—Scarabus has imprisoned her."

Dr. Bedlo grunted. "We'll get her out right now," he said, and forthwith, he started leading Rexford toward the hallway door.

"Then," Dr. Bedlo continued, his hand gripping the knob, "I want you to take her away from here as quickly as you can."

"What about her father?" Rexford asked.

"Let me worry about that," Adolphus Bedlo told him, and giving him no chance either to question or to protest this dictum, he opened the door and went out.

Rexford followed him. Then, side by side, walking slowly, and making as little noise as possible, they moved without incident to the end of the corridor. But, just as Rexford was beginning to turn the corner, Dr. Bedlo grabbed at his arm and tugged him back.

Rexford goggled at him for a moment. And for a moment, Rexford almost cried out. Then both Bedlos stood still, listening. And both peered tensely around the edge of the wall.

Lenore and Dr. Scarabus were approaching down the main hallway. And Lenore, who was wearing a long robe, was carrying in her left hand a lighted candle, the flame of which she was shading with her right, directing it so that it cast a pale glow not only about her feet but also a considerable distance ahead of them.

Again, Dr. Bedlo tugged at Rexford, moving him now to a

window alcove on the opposite side of the hall. After he had pushed Rexford in, he leaned forward and whispered to him, "You'll hide here. Then, as soon as Dr. Scarabus has passed, you'll release Miss Craven from her room and get her out of this castle."

"What about *you?*"

"*Never mind me!*" Dr. Bedlo hissed at him. "Do as I tell you!" Suddenly, with a quite unexpected and thoroughly unprecedented show of affection, he reached up and ran his hand through Rexford's hair. Then he said in a voice that was almost gentle, "For once in your life?" And hastily, he drew the drapes over the alcove, cutting off Rexford's attempted reply.

"*Don't make a sound,*" he hissed before, turning, he scurried back along the corridor and into the room that he and Rexford had just left.

Holding his breath, Rexford peered out from behind the drapes, watching for Dr. Scarabus and Lenore. And within the instant, he saw the glow of Lenore's candle as it preceded them around the corner. An instant later they had passed him, had moved down the corridor, and had stopped—Rexford's face contorted with shock as he realized it—in front of the very door through which Dr. Bedlo had disappeared.

Dr. Scarabus opened the door and held it for Lenore. Then, entering the room after her, he shut the door in his wake. And now the hallway was clear.

Rexford came out of the alcove immediately. But for several moments he could do no more than stand before the drapes, his expression one of painful indecision as he look first this way, then that.

Finally, he started toward the door.

But he stopped after he had taken scarcely a dozen paces. He had to save Estelle. Turning, he raced down the hallway in the direction of her room.

"Well, look who's here," Lenore said, seeing Adolphus Bedlo regarding her and Dr. Scarabus from the depths of a large chair on the other side of the room.

Bedlo said nothing. Dr. Scarabus said nothing.

And Lenore, after putting her candle on the nearer of the two tables that flanked the door, gazed at Dr. Scarabus in mute admiration for a moment, then replied to his impassive smile by shrugging her shoulders and saying, "I should have known—you sly old man, you."

Still silent, and still smiling, Dr. Scarabus motioned her across the room and to a chair. He waited until she was comfortably seated. Then he, too, crossed the room.

As he was about to settle himself into the chair next to hers, Lenore asked, with a pointed glance from him to Dr. Scarabus, then back again to him, "And what, my dear, was our friend's price?"

"A double value, madame." It was Bedlo himself who answered her.

She looked at him.

And although he was grossly offended by her attitude, he managed yet to wring a smile from his lips. "I am to gain, first superior magical power—and then, via my convenient 'death' by lightning—*freedom from overbearing women.*"

"Well worth the cost of being turned into an insignificant bird," Lenore said, acidly sweet.

"*And,*" Dr. Scarabus added, "luring Dr. Craven to me. Do not forget that part, my precious ogress."

Dr. Bedlo retained his smile for another moment. Then, while Lenore was returning her attention to Dr. Scarabus, he glanced covertly toward the hall. After which, looking vastly pleased with himself, he sand back into the recesses of his chair.

"I can't imagine," Lenore said coldly, "why you could want Erasmus here."

"It is not *him* I want." Dr. Scarabus' expression was now neither affable nor impassive. Like his voice, it was totally ruthless. "*It is his magic.*"

Hurrying up to Estelle's room, Rexford quickly threw back the bolts and opened the door.

Inside, Estelle turned, startled. Then, seeing who it was, she smiled in relief. "Thank heaven you're all right," she said softly, and moved forward to meet him

He stayed in the open doorway, gesturing at her to make haste. When she was close enough, he reached out, and grasping her hand, half led her, half pulled her from the room.

"Where are we going?" Estelle asked, gasping slightly as they approached the staircase.

Out of here," Rexford said.

Abruptly, she jerked her hand away from his and cam to a stubborn halt. "Without my father?"

"Estelle," Rexford said pleadingly, we've got to leave—and *now*. It's too dangerous—"

Clutching at his head, Rexford groaned feelingly—as if he knew in advance how disastrous Estelle's delay was going to be.

Chapter 12

WAS HE insane? Temporarily insane? Under an enchantment? And Lenore—had what he had seen—*yes,* seen—had this been a mere hallucination? And evil trick? An apparition formed out of wind and rain, urgent need and strong desire?

Erasmus Craven didn't know. And now, he no longer wanted to know.

He was lying on the bed in his room, staring up at the ceiling, its molding, it grinning seraphim, and its fat, smirking cherubs. He didn't hear the door open, nor did he hear Estelle and Rexford enter from the hallway and come across the room to stand at his side. Estelle reached down, and very gently, she shook his shoulder. Only then did he stir, sit up, gaze vacantly at her and Rexford.

"We're leaving, Father," she said quickly, urgently.

"Leaving?" he echoed dully. He looked at her, looked at the hand she was now holding out to him, shook his head.

"I've been locked in my room. Rexford here had to—" Estelle stopped suddenly. She drew back her hand. "What is it, Father?" she asked, frightened, pale.

"I saw Lenore." He said it lifelessly, without conviction, without tone, and again, he shook his head.

"You—?" Estelle could say no more. She stared at her father, wondering—as he himself had wondered—whether he had gone mad.

"Please," Rexford said, and touched her arm impatiently. "Father said we had to leave as soon as possible."

Estelle whirled about, and Dr. Craven, starting momentarily, then looked up with a new confusion.

"*Yes,*" Rexford breathed. He's still alive. His apparent death was just a trick to feel Dr. Scarabus. Now, *please!*" He gazed at Estelle, motioned toward the door. "We've got to go."

Estelle nodded. Then, turning once more, she pulled Dr. Craven to his feet, and taking his right arm while Rexford too his left, led him to the door. Dr. Craven came docilely, shaking his head, looking lost.

Dr. Bedlo glanced toward the hallway again, then sat forward in shock reached out to Lenore.

"Come," Dr. Scarabus was saying. "It is time."

"One moment," Dr. Bedlo said on impulse.

Dr. Scarabus looked at him through narrowing eyes, watching him squirm in his chair as he groped for words—any words, as long as they used up time.

"I don't believe you quite appreciate what I've been through," the fat man managed at last. "You might have warned me how completely inadequate black feathers are to keep a body warm on a December night."

Dr. Scarabus started to speak.

But Bedlo cut him off, complaining on. "You might also have warned me about hawks. I was attacked *three* times before I got to Craven's house—only to discover that he didn't have the slightest notion how to turn me back into a man!"

"A *man?*" Lenore said, eyeing him scornfully.

Dr. Bedlo was now caught up in his topic. He ignored her, continued, "If I hadn't known the formula for reconversion, I'd *still* be a raven."

"I liked you better that way," Lenore said, and considering that the conversation had been thus put to its end, she began to push herself from her chair.

Dr. Craven, Rexford on his left, and Estelle on his right were starting down the staircase, moving stealthily but at an acceptable

96

pace. They were going to get away.

Suddenly, Dr. Craven stopped, pulled loose from his rescuers, "I must save Dr. Bedlo," he said.

"Sir," Rexford said, pleadingly, "he told me not to—"

But Dr. Craven was on the top step now, and now he was beginning to move down the hallway.

With a groan, Rexford hurried after him, grabbed him.

"Then"—Dr. Adolphus Bedlo waved his hands, spoke wildly—"to top it all, I am almost *chopped* to pieces on the rocks by my own son!" He glowered at Dr. Scarabus, challenging him to explain.

Dr. Scarabus regarded him narrowly for another moment. Then, leaning toward him, he asked, "Are you quite finished?"

Dr. Bedlo opened his mouth and raised his hands as if to go on.

But Dr. Scarabus was already saying, "You *are.*" And Dr. Scarabus was looking at him in a way that suggested, strongly suggested, it would be best for him to abandon the subject—and to seek for no other.

Accordingly, the ever prudent little fat man lapsed, silent, back to the depths of his chair.

Dr. Scarabus turned again to Lenore. "It is time for me to be acquiring Dr. Craven's secret," he told her.

"Are you going to torture him?" Lenore asked with pleasurable anticipation.

"That won't be necessary now," he said, and smiled. *"I have his daughter."*

"Oh," Dr. Bedlo said, to stunned to pretend well. "Yes. That's a—*very* good idea." He sat up, grinning sickly, tapping his plump fingertips together, and trying to meet Dr. Scarabus' eyes.

And suddenly, Dr. Scarabus sprang to his feet, glared suspiciously at Bedlo for an instant, then, darting out his hand, caught Bedlo around the throat and pulled him close.

"Wh—what are you doing?" Dr. Bedlo asked nervously as Dr. Scarabus, holding him, now peered intently into his eyes.

Dr. Scarabus slapped him once, hard. Then, as quickly as he had seized him, he hurled him away, and whirling, rushed toward the door.

Lenore looked after him in surprise. Then she stood up, followed him out of the room.

Dr. Bedlo, sprawling on the floor near his chair, shut his eyes for a moment. When he was able to look up, he saw that Lenore and Dr. Scarabus had gone. The door was standing wide. He struggled to rise.

Dr. Craven, and Estelle and Rexford, who were once again supporting his either side, had almost reached the front door. A few more steps, then open it, and they would be safe.

Dr. Scarabus, his face a mask of impending fury, turned the corner and raced down the main hallway, heading for the stairs. Lenore was not far behind him. Dr. Bedlo was a feeble and panting last.

As he came to the railing that was the start of the upstairs balcony, Dr. Scarabus jerked to a halt and stared across it, down the entry hall—and at the three who were about to make good their escape. He raised his right arm dramatically, and he held it high for a moment while he pointed downward with the index finger of his left hand. Then, his nostrils pinching and flaring, his eyes glittering evilly, the beginnings of a smile twitching at the corners of his mouth, he slashed down the arm, drew it back a bit, and stiffening it, circled widely with his flattened right hand.

Lenore gasped. She could see the gestures, but she could not yet see their objects. Then, coming to Dr. Scarabus' side, she looked down, gasped again, and at last, smiled viciously, delightedly.

Dr. Craven, Estelle, and Rexford had gained the door, it had disappeared and become part of the wall. Estelle had turned and looked up at her father, expecting him to help.

"Father, you've got to—" She broke off.

And now she was screaming in horror.

Rexford, who had been frantically examining the wall, whirled around, then stood still, dumbfounded, gaping at Dr. Craven, and staring at him in brute dismay.

Or rather, Rexford was staring at a marble statue, cold and rigid, dressed as Dr. Craven had been dressed, standing where Dr. Craven had been standing, and bearing Dr. Craven's features, frozen—possibly forever—in an expression that was at once stupid and surprised, confused, and deeply, hopelessly terrified.

"*Good,*" Dr. Bedlo said, faking poorly. He had now joined the smiling Scarabus, the smiling Lenore, and like these two, he was looking down at the entry hall and at those who were trapped in it. "You've captured them," he said to Dr. Scarabus. Then he tried to smile.

And Dr. Scarabus, turning to him, studied him with venomous eyes for a moment. Then, once again, he gestured, but this gesture was the merest flick of the thumb and forefinger of his right hand in Bedlo's direction. It was enough.

Suddenly, Dr. Adolphus Bedlo was bound from his neck to his ankles with heavy rope. "What's this?" he asked, lightly he hoped, and he wrinkled his nose as if ready to enjoy some hilarious jest with Dr. Scarabus, and Dr. Scarabus alone.

Lenore glanced contemptuously at the trussed up little sorcerer. Then she looked at Dr. Scarabus, waited for him to explain this new turn of events. Dr. Scarabus smiled gently at her, patted the top of her ebony head, and said nothing.

Meanwhile, Dr. Adolphus Bedlo was getting distinctly uncomfortable. He wiggled, and wiggled again, and frowning discovered that he had only tightened himself into the coils of rope. Now the rope chafed miserably at his wrists, his throat, his ankles and knees. Frightened now, he whimpered softly. Then, stopping himself, and doing his best to appear indignant, he demanded of Dr. Scarabus, "Is this how you reward my services to you?"

Dr. Scarabus grinned hideously. "Fear not," he said in a ponderous and awesome tone. "You shall receive your just reward."

Dr. Bedlo looked at him in mortal dread.

Below, Estelle Craven, whose screaming had subsided into choking gasps of terror, and Rexford Bedlo, who had finally managed, with the expenditure of untold effort, to blink at Estelle and then to grip her hand, stared up at the balcony, at their two captors, and at the fellow captive. Then, gazing at each other, they awaited their fate.

Dr. Erasmus Craven's eyes were yellow marble, streaked through with fine blue-brown veins. He could see nothing. His ears were of the same substance. He could not hear. His expression remained just as it had been—puzzled and surprised and dumbly, dazedly horrified.

Chapter 13

THE WALLS of the great stone dungeon were ranged with implements of torture—whips of every description, pinchers and knives, cuffs, boot, and a variety of strange devices forged for purposes to hideous to speculate upon. One section of wall was, however, bare of everything but the flaming torches that lighted it. Here there had been array of iron branding rods.

These rods were now in the center of the cavernous chamber, their thick handles protruding from all four sides of a huge pit of glowing coals.

Gort, a deaf-mute with the posture and the body of a gorilla, the expression and the face of a long-fanged wild boar, had withdrawn one of the shorter rods and was now holding it up for his master's approval.

Dr. Scarabus grunted, then gestured slightly with his head.

Obediently, Gort extended the palm of his left hand, and without hesitation, lowered the rod and pressed its spitting white-hot face into his flesh.

There was a ghastly hissing sound; there was a curl of acrid smoke; there was the stench of charring flesh. Gort quivered tautly—no more. Then he pressed the rod deeper, staring the while at his master. And then after several moments, he drew the rod away; he grinned; and he displayed his palm to Dr. Scarabus.

The old sorcerer inspected it dispassionately. Then he shook his head, pointed at the rod, and mumbled to himself, "It's not quite ready yet." He signaled to Gort, and smiling now, he watched Gort slide the rod back into the coals.

Gort remained beside the pit. Occasionally, he stirred at the coals with one or another of the rods that were heating in them. Occasionally, he squatted at one or another edge of the pit and blew into and over the coals, blowing harder and harder as his boar's face reddened and shined and blazed from the intense heat.

Dr. Scarabus paced the floor of the dungeon. Once in a while he looked at the coals, the rods, and Gort. Once in a while he looked toward the lower door, through which Lenore was due to appear as soon as she had changed from her robe, rearranged her hair, and done whatever other little chores she considered necessary. Once in a while he looked up, and at these times, he invariably smiled.

A long balcony jutted over one side of the torture chamber proper. It was at this balcony that Dr. Scarabus smiled, for there were thirteen dark and narrow cells opening onto it, and in the center cell, which was locked, were Dr. Scarabus' guests—Estelle Craven, with her hands roped to the wall above her head, Rexford Bedlo, next to her and in a similar position, and Drs. Adolphus Bedlo and Erasmus Craven, bound hand and foot and lying as apart on the floor as its restricted area would permit.

The four prisoners had smelled the smell of burning flesh. The had listened to Dr. Scarabus' footsteps, and those of Gort, resounding hollowly on the stones below. But they could see nothing of what was beyond the cell, and no words were spoken for them to overhear.

They could only guess at what was happening, guess at what would be their fate—guess and tremble, and in Dr. Bedlo's case, whimper also.

After a long while, Estelle sighed, then asked, "Can't you get your hands free, Father?"

Dr. Craven turned his eyes to her. "I'm afraid not, my dear," he said. "Dr. Scarabus has seen to that—first changing me into a statue—then binding me like this."

Estelle sighed again and said no more.

Rexford Bedlo was staring gloomily at the floor, and now and then, staring at Adolphus Bedlo in disgust. As Rexford started to speak, the elder Bedlo glanced up at him and said, cutting him off, "Don't bother—I know. I'm a disgrace."

"I had a somewhat stronger word in mind," Rexford answered tightly.

"Try to understand me, Rexford," Dr. Bedlo said.

"What is there to understand?" Rexford smiled down at him. It was a thin smile, and a very bitter one.

"Why I did it." The elder Bedlo paused for a moment, tried to take the whining note out of his voice. "All my life I've been of little consequence. Everything I ever tried—I failed at."

Rexford looked at him, as did Dr. Craven and Estelle. No one was smiling now.

"That's why I turned to magic," Dr. Bedlo continued. "Hoping to find, in it, an answer to my lack of purpose—a meaning to my life."

He gazed at Dr. Craven, then went on, speaking now primarily to him, "A subversive of the natural; true enough. Not worthy of desire. Except to men like Scarabus and myself. Men upon whom nature has bestowed the souls of toads."

Dr. Craven was no longer angry with Bedlo. He looked at him, trying to show that he was sympathetic—and to conceal the fact that he was distinctly uncomfortable.

Rexford and Estelle looked away; then they fixed their eyes on each other. Both were puzzled by Dr. Bedlo's self recriminations. Neither was certain how to react to them.

Dr. Bedlo sniffled. Then he made himself stop, grin.

"When Scarabus invited me to join the Brotherhood of Sorcerers—I thought myself the happiest man alive." He grinned once again, crookedly now, sadly, and as if in torment. And looking now at Rexford, he spoke in a tone of plea. "The invitation came, of course, because he sensed, in me, the makings of a perfect lackey. Very soon, I sat directly at his right hand—fawning and obedient—ever and always, ready to obey. I was as grateful as a mongrel for any scrap of favor he might deign to toss before me.

"When he offered me, in return for luring Dr. Craven here, not only added skill at magic but freedom from your mother as well—I embraced the opportunity. You mother never loved me, Rexford. And I lost my love for her when I realized that she regarded our marriage as an unfortunate mistake."

"That isn't true," Rexford said defensively.

"It *is* true," the elder Bedlo insisted. "She never admitted it, of course; she never would. She chose, instead, to become a tyrant toward me, releasing her distaste for me through nagging and through criticism—until I could take no more."

Rexford said nothing.

And Dr. Bedlo, dropping his eyes, closed them in shame for a moment. Then he turned to Dr. Craven, and looking at him, said softly, humbly, "I know there is no meaning to it now, but—with all my heart—I tell you that I am truly sorry for what I did to you. And to your daughter."

"And to your son? Dr. Craven asked.

"Would that he were my son," Dr. Bedlo said glumly. *"Look* at him—slender—tall—of fine appearance." Adolphus Bedlo watched Dr. Craven's eyes turn to Rexford, and at last, he forced his own eyes to follow them. He stared at Rexford then, and grimacing, he asked, "How could *I* be his father? What could *I* sire but more monstrosities like myself?"

"Father—" Rexford interrupted, sympathetic.

"Don't *call* me that! Dr. Bedlo averted his face. "I'm your *step-father*—nothing more."

Once again, Rexford was silent.

And Dr. Craven, too, was silent for a moment. Then, sighing, he gazed at Adolphus Bedlo and said quietly, "You are not alone in guilt, sir."

"What?" Dr. Bedlo looked at him in confusion.

"I, too, have failed at the task of living," Dr. Craven said. "Instead of facing it, I turned my back on it. I retreated—*hid*—ignored my father's wishes. I refused to accept the responsibility that was mine by inheritance—choosing, instead, convenience—comfort.

"I know now why my father resisted Scarabus even at the cost of his health—perhaps, of his life. Because he knew that evil cannot be fought by hiding from it. Men like Scarabus thrive on the apathy of others.

"He has thrived on mine. By avoiding contact with the Brotherhood, I have given him the freedom to commit his savageries unopposed."

Dr. Craven had finished. He lowered his eyes in silent self-condemnation. He could say no more. Nor could Dr. Bedlo, or Rexford, or Estelle, find any words that were appropriate to his grief.

Suddenly, however, all heard the sound of applause. All looked toward the door of the cell. And then the three others looked quickly away from it, back to Dr. Craven, who was gasping, gagging, deathly pale.

"Bravo, Erasmus," Lenore said, and smiled sweetly at him. She was standing just outside the door, leaning against its grillwork in such a way as to appear casual, yet not to disarrange either her carefully ordered masses of clack curls or the delicate fold of her blue silk gown.

He could only gape, and goggle, and gasp at her.

"*Splendid* dissertation," she said, and she smiled again.

"Lenore—" he whispered, barely able to form even that sound.

In her hand was the key to the cell. She tapped it on the grillwork, listened to it clang. Then, after a moment, she inserted and turned it in the lock, opened the cell door, and moved to her husband's side.

"You look about the same," she said, eyeing him coolly. Then, nodding toward Estelle without looking at her, she shrugged and added, "So does the girl."

Dr. Craven blinked. "You—you're *alive*," he stammered.

"Oh course I'm alive," Lenore said. "That was someone else's body in my casket. I left you for Scarabus."

"*No*" Erasmus Craven was stunned.

Lenore was enjoying herself. She smiled.

"What has Scarabus done to you?" her husband asked fervently. "Are you under a spell?"

"The spell of *greed.*" It was Dr. Bedlo who answered.

Lenore, much amused by this, laughed softly, melodiously.

Her eyes remained on Dr. Craven. They glittered wildly, narrowing a little as she laughed, then opening very wide to tease Erasmus Craven and to envelop him in their black and boundless scorn.

"*Lenore,*" he said, begging her. "My love. Please. *Speak* to me."

You're as much of a bore as ever, aren't you, Erasmus?" She gazed down at him as if she had just done him an enormous favor.

For a moment, he looked at her with the expression of a wounded child. Then, wincing, he shut his eyes. And he moaned slowly and feebly, without any spirit and without any strength.

Lenore shook her head over him. "How I could stand to live

with you as long as I did is totally beyond me, she said acidly.

Once more, he moaned—but just once more.

For now Dr. Scarabus had entered the cell, and Gort was entering it behind him.

"I believe that we are ready to begin now, gentlemen," Dr. Scarabus said.

Everyone looked at him.

"*No,*" Dr. Bedlo whimpered, panicking.

"You disagree?" Dr. Scarabus asked tauntingly.

And Adolphus Bedlo pleaded, *"Let me go, Scarabus."* His eyes were wet with tears. "I'll do anything you say. Just don't hurt me."

"Father—!" Rexford Bedlo said, pained, and deeply shocked.

"Let me go," Dr. Adolphus Bedlo whined on, ignoring him. "Please let me go."

Dr. Scarabus smiled. "But what about your friends?" he asked equably.

"They are no friends of mine!" Dr. Bedlo said, turning savage. "Do what you want with them!"

"And with your son as well?"

"He's not of my blood! Let him *die!* What do *I* care!"

"Dr. Bedlo—!" Erasmus Craven said. He looked at him appealing to him, suffering at the sight of his ignominious display.

But Dr. Bedlo paid him no heed. "Scarabus," he said, whining still, "I beg of you! Release me!"

Dr. Scarabus only smiled at him.

"All right! Turn me back into a raven then. Throw me out into the night! Even hawks and freezing cold are better than death!" He sobbed pitifully. "Please!" he said, whining again. "I *beg of* you!"

Lenore was standing beside Dr. Scarabus now. She, too, was smiling. "It might be more amusing," she said softly.

Dr. Scarabus looked at her. Then he looked closely at Bedlo, and genuinely curious, he asked him, "And you don't care about the others?"

"To *hell* with the others!"

Dr. Craven averted his face, and Rexford and Estelle lowered their heads. All three were embarrassed, hurt. All three were almost crushed by shame.

Dr. Scarabus was nodding to himself. "I must admit, he said after a moment of consideration, "that the depth of such treachery fills me with unbounded admiration. And—since Dr. Craven will never have the opportunity of helping you again—"

He considered a moment more. Then, abruptly, he gestured, flicking the thumb and forefinger of his right hand toward Dr. Bedlo, waving the hand over him, then pulling it sharply back.

Where Adolphus Bedlo had been there was now a mound of tangled ropes. Perched upon them was a raven, glossy and ugly and black. "Thank you!" it said, speaking with Bedlo's voice.

Dr. Scarabus shrugged depreciatorily. It was nothing. He smiled again, as did Lenore. Both were vastly amused.

The three who remained prisoners stared at the bird, shocked. They thought, not of themselves, but of Dr. Bedlo—and Dr. Bedlo's perfidy.

But the raven gave them never a word, never even a glance. Spreading its wings, it flew upward and came to light on the sill of a high, slitlike window. *"Thank you!"* it called once more, and with that, it soared out and disappeared into the stormy night.

"And so," Dr. Scarabus said cheerfully, "farewell to Dr. Bedlo— as he flaps to his well-deserved oblivion."

Then, looking away from the window, he fixed his eyes on those of Dr. Craven, and grinning broadly, said to him, "And now for you, dear doctor."

His eyes were still on Craven's as he motioned to Gort, nodding to indicate what he wanted done. When he spoke it was for Dr. Craven's benefit rather than for that of the deaf-mute. "Take the young lady below."

"What?" Dr. Craven said faintly, as he watched in mounting horror as Gort cut Estelle's bonds and led her forcibly toward the door of the cell.

Estelle looked pleadingly at her father.

But he was powerless. He couldn't move his hands, couldn't help her. "What are you doing?" he said, looking from her to Dr. Scarabus.

The old sorcerer only smiled.

"What are you doing?"

Dr. Scarabus turned silently. He waited until Gort had pushed Estelle through the door. Then he signaled to Lenore, and after waiting again, followed her out of the cell.

"Scarabus, you swine!" Rexford Bedlo shouted at his departing back. Like Dr. Craven, Rexford was struggling to free himself. Like Dr. Craven, he was having no success.

"Estelle," Dr. Craven groaned, stricken.

He breathed hard for several moments. Then gathering all his strength, and holding his breath to conserve it, he fought once more against the bonds, but to no avail. He stared at the door, stared at Rexford in dismay. "Oh for my hands," he said tightly, desperately. *"My hands."*

Rexford had cast his eyes toward the floor. He didn't answer—except perhaps with a small gasp of agony.

Now Dr. Craven, too, cast down his eyes.

Neither he nor Rexford looked up until, a short while later, Gort came back into the cell. Then Rexford gasped again, watching the brutish servant go to Dr. Craven, haul him to his feet, and drag him toward the cell door. And again, watching him shove Dr. Craven, still bound, out of the cell and against the balcony wall.

Dr. Craven's back was now propped against the wall, and Gort was holding him thus, and thus forcing him to look down at the torture chamber below, at the pit of glowing coals and the rods that protruded from it, and at Estelle whose wrists had been clamped inside a pair of wall manacles, whose clothes had been ripped away from her heaving bosom—Estelle, who was staring upward, helpless and in terror.

Dr. Scarabus and Lenore were also looking up. Both were smiling at him.

"And now, dear doctor," Scarabus said casually, I offer you a choice. The secret of your hand manipulations—*or"*— he jerked one of the rods out of the coals and held it up— *"this*—against" —and moving over to Estelle, he held the white-hot face of the iron close, close to the side of her neck—*"This."*

"No—" Dr. Craven said faintly.

"Do not tell him, Father! " Estelle called out despite her fear. "You know to what evil ends he would put your secret!"

She gazed up at her father's tormented face, his uncertainty, his dread. Dr. Scarabus had returned the rod to the coals. But now his hand was on another rod, larger, and nearer to the center of the pit.

"Please," Estelle called out, pleading. "Let me die. Let me die rather than know what the secret was lost because of me!"

Dr. Scarabus looked up, smiled once more. "Is that your wish as well, dear doctor?"

Chapter 14

ALONE IN the cell, with his hands still lashed above him, Rexford Bedlo had slumped forward in surrender. He was aware of the painful throbbing in his arms, and dimly, he was aware of the painful throbbing in his arms, and dimly, he was aware of the voices that rose to the cell from the great hollow that was just beyond its door. Hours seemed to be elapsing. He was exhausted. Yet consciousness refused to leave him. For he knew that someone—someone he cared about—was in mortal danger.

Suddenly, a succession of flapping noises made Rexford jerk back his head and look toward the window. The raven was perched on the sill, shaking the raindrops from its wings. Rexford stared at it, not knowing what to say, not knowing what to expect.

After a moment, the bird flitted down, and coming to light on the top of Rexford's head, began pecking at the ropes that held him.

Rexford smiled in sudden relief and joy. "You *didn't* run away," He whispered

The bird stopped pecking. "Is that what you thought?" it asked in a hurt tone. Then started pecking again.

"What else could I—?"

"All *right*," the bird interrupted. "Never mind."

It went on pecking at Rexford's bonds, stopping only once, and then only long enough to remark irritable, "He might have given me a sharper beak."

Dr. Scarabus had withdrawn another white-hot iron from the coals. Holding it beside Estelle's neck, he was looking up at Dr. Craven. "I can wait no longer, doctor," he said. "Perhaps the sight of your daughter's flesh being cooked will clarify your thinking."

Dr. Craven stared down at him, at Estelle, and at the cruelly smiling Lenore. Torn between his instinct to save his child and the realization that he dare not accede to Scarabus' demands, he trembled, weeping openly, and alternately nodding and shaking his head. He could not decide.

The raven had finished pecking through Rexford's bonds, and now Rexford was able to pull himself loose. Slipping the rope from his wrists, he ran now to the cell door. The bird hopped from his head to his shoulder, perched there.

By peering around the edge of the doorway, Rexford could see Dr. Craven—and Gort, who was guarding him. Reaching back into the cell, Rexford seized up a heavy stool. Then he braced himself for action, lunged through the doorway, and smashed the stool over Gort's head.

There was a dull thus, and Gort dropped to the floor of the balcony, Rexford dropping with him, falling on top of him, fighting him. Both he and Gort were behind the balcony rail, out of view of those in the dungeon below. But Dr. Craven was staring down in shock, watching the two who were struggling near his feet.

"Don't look!" Rexford whispered urgently.

Dr. Craven turned his eyes again to the torture chamber.

Too late. Scarabus, about to burn Estelle's neck, had glanced up at him to say, "Your final chance, dear doc—" Then he had broken off, frowning with sudden suspicion.

"Gort?" he was asking now.

He looked up at Dr. Craven, glowering at him for a moment before he turned to Lenore and asked, "Where is Gort?"

Lenore shook her head. She didn't know.

And now, hidden behind the balcony rail, Rexford had subdued Gort; Gort was unconscious, and Rexford had Gort's knife in his hand. He crawled over to Dr. Craven, and staying low, began to slice through his bonds.

Dr. Craven's face was expressionless. But now he was no longer dazed. Now he was no longer confused.

Suddenly, his hands were free. And suddenly he lifted them up to gesture.

Dr. Scarabus gasped, and dropping the branding rod, he raised his own hands to gesture.

The two sorcerers glared at each other for an instant. Then they gestured—simultaneously.

And the black lightning shooting up from Dr. Scarabus' fingers collided head-on with the white lighting shooting down from Dr. Craven's. The was a quick, sharp crackling; there was a loud explosion; and then there were echoes. Both lightnings vanished.

Once again, the two sorcerers glared at each other. For a moment, all was suspended, waiting. Then, abruptly, Dr. Scarabus swept his arms to either side, gesturing.

Twin streaks of black lightning started swiftly toward the balcony, curving inward so that they would meet at Erasmus Craven's body.

But Dr. Craven had also swept his arms out. And as the streaks of black lightning were about to converge upon him, they were met and explosively destroyed by two of his own lightning streaks.

Dr. Scarabus' face distorted with fury as he glared at Dr. Craven for another suspended moment. At last, overlapping his flatted hands in front of his chest, he then moved them outward in a rapid fanning gesture.

A tremendous wave of dark power surged toward Dr. Craven—who was, by now, making a gesture exactly like that which Scarabus had made.

Both men kept their hands tensely raised. And the black power of Scarabus met and undulated against Erasmus Craven's wave of white. Abruptly, the two waves of power stiffened. Then, for several moments, they pressed close in the air and ground violently against each other.

But neither could conquer.

And now the strength of each was beginning to diminish. Both waves were beginning to evaporate. Both were almost gone.

Dr. Scarabus lowered his hands. Momentarily, they were drained of force. Dr. Craven, also weakened for the moment, lowered his hands too.

"Enough," Scarabus said at last. "This is no answer."

"*Is* there an answer then?" Dr. Craven asked.

"Yes," Scarabus told him, smiling grimly now, "A duel—*to the death.*"

Dr. Craven was silent, frowning, unwilling to consent.

"There is no other way, doctor," the other man said darkly. "Resign yourself to that. The conflict in inevitable. You and I can no longer coexist in a condition of stalemate." He paused for a moment, glowering. Then he said, *"One of us must perish."*

And still, Dr. Craven was silent. Hating duels—hating all violence, whatever its nature, whatever its cause—he wished more than anything to refuse Dr. Scarabus' challenge. Yet, how could he. He had to save Estelle, Rexford. Himself.

And what of his responsibility? The obligation of his inheritance? Had he spoken falsely when he was bound and helpless on the floor of the cell? Had he lied to himself then just as he had been lying to himself for so many rutile years? Had he lied to Estelle, whose belief in him was so strong that she was willing to be tortured to death before she abandoned it? Did he really think that he could forever hide from evil?

Dr. Scarabus was smiling up at him, waiting for his answer.

And drawing in a slow breath, Dr. Erasmus Craven stood up straight. "Very well," he said. "A duel then. *To the death.*"

Chapter 15

A LARGE OVAL had been cleared in the center of the entry hall, and at the ends of this arena, two empty chairs waited for the contestants to appear.

Above, looking down from the balcony on the bedroom floor, were Estelle Craven, Rexford Bedlo, and the raven, which was perched on Rexford's shoulder.

Lenore sat on the top step of the great spiral staircase. She had changed clothes in honor of the coming spectacle, and was now wearing a billowy white ball gown, artfully and immodestly cut. A crimson lace shawl did little to keep her warm in the predawn chill—Lenore never needed to be kept warm—but it contributed much to the effect of her dress.

She smiled enigmatically when a rear door opened and Craven and Scarabus entered the hall to take their respective places. Estelle leaned forward anxiously, and at the same time, reached for Rexford's hand. The raven hopped down to the balcony rail, then back to Rexford's shoulder; down, then back; repeating the process several times while the contestants moved to their scars, when finally settling itself on Rexford's shoulder again.

Dr. Scarabus' expression was hard, concentrated. Dr. Craven, although clearly worried, had the manner of an expert—prepared to do his all, and eventually, to conquer. He composed himself in his chair, lightly rested his hands on the arms, and proceeded to gaze steadily at the aged necromancer who was his opponent.

Dr. Scarabus sat in an identical position and quietly returned Craven's gaze.

For several moments, neither man moved.

Then, very slowly, the index finger of Dr. Scarabus' right hand flexed up from the arm of the chair. Dr. Craven stiffened. The finger rose, uncurled, pointed at him.

And a dark, banded snake wrapped itself tightly around his neck.

Erasmus Craven's right hand made a slight brushing motion.

Instead of the snake, a dark scarf with gay red and yellow stripes was now around his neck. Keeping his eyes on Scarabus, he slowly unwound it, rolled it into a thick ball between his hands, and almost casually, lobbed it across the space that separated him from the other magician.

Dr. Scarabus watched, smiling faintly as the scarf came toward him.

Suddenly, he winced. A black bat was clinging against the side of his neck. His right hand clutched at it, and after a moment, drew it away. It had become a black fan.

Fanning himself with it, Dr. Scarabus deliberated his next move, taking his time, but never relaxing his surveillance of the man opposite. Apart from the hardness in his eyes, the elder sorcerer's face was virtually without expression. On his neck, a small bite dribbled blood. With the index finger of his left hand he touched the blood; then, raising the finger before his eyes, he inspected it—coldly, and without letting Dr. Craven from his watch.

Dr. Craven, too, was watching, and his face, too, was expressionless and wooden. He had decided to confine himself to defense for the time being. Later he would become more familiar with Dr. Scarabus' methods.

Still fanning, Dr. Scarabus lowered his finger and put his hand in his lap.

Dr. Craven looked at him, saw him, after a few moments, stop fanning and bring the open fan down to his lap, thereby hiding his left hand.

Beneath the fan, Dr. Scarabus gestured with his left hand.

Dr. Craven's gaze flicked down, then up. And very quickly now, he chopped downward with his flatted right hand, causing a plan of solid color—it was blue—to form in front of him and deflect the dagger that was hurtling toward his heart. As the dagger clattered harmlessly to the floor, he gestured again and another plane—a green one—formed in another place. Another dagger bounced backward and fell to rest.

Three times more—red, purple, violet—this process was repeated. Five daggers lay on the floor about Dr. Craven's chair. Five planes of color, one overlapping the other, hung in the air before it.

Dr. Scarabus seemed to be on the verge of irritation. A muscle quivered at one corner of his mouth. Two veins stood out blue and throbbing on his temples. Brusquely, he discarded the fan, gestured with his right hand.

And Dr. Craven, using both flatted hands, gestured from front to back, up, over and around his head—which was now surrounded by a thick transparent dome. The blade of a giant ax was buried in the top of this dome, plainly visible, but distorted by its curvature.

After several moments, Dr. Craven made the gesture of a man brushing away a gnat, and everything—knives, planes, dome, and ax—disappeared.

Whereupon Dr. Scarabus, definitely irritated now, muttered something under his breath, then hooked and extended the first three fingers of his right hand.

The mouth of a large cannon faced Dr. Craven. The cannon's fuse sizzled noisily. There was a deafening explosion.

Dr. Craven snapped his fingers.

And the cannon ball gloated lazily toward the ceiling, drifted for a while in the same way that a black balloon might drift, and then, picking up speed, headed back toward Dr. Scarabus.

Muttering angrily, Dr. Scarabus gestured.

And just before the cannon ball would have hit his head, it stopped. It hovered for an instant. Then it was stationary in the air above him.

Dr. Craven snapped his fingers.

As if it were a paper toy constructed for just this purpose, the cannon ball popped apart, spraying Dr. Scarabus with bright multicolored confetti.

Sitting on the stairs, Lenore frowned; she was annoyed, very annoyed. Standing about, Estelle and Rexford smiled, and Estelle gave Rexford's hand a quick and happy squeeze; they were relieved.

And perched on Rexford's shoulder, the delighted raven spread its wings and hollered, "Touché! You Old—!"

The competing magicians had been gazing at each other without a sound. Suddenly Dr. Scarabus had gestured. Suddenly there was a deep snarl, a menacing animal growl.

Dr. Craven glanced to his right—and saw an enormous mastiff. A new growl was rumbling in its throat. It was slavering; its teeth were bared. It was ready to spring.

Dr. Craven lifted his hand to gesture, Dr. Scarabus gestured again. Dr. Craven's hand froze in mid-air. He glanced to his left—and saw a second mastiff, every bit as ugly as the first. It, too, was growling, slavering, poised to spring.

Suddenly, a third dog growled, this one in front of Dr. Craven. And a fourth, which was behind him. He was surrounded now, ringed in by four dogs, all growling, slavering, crouched to leap.

Dr. Scarabus smiled cruelly. He gestured. And the four mastiffs attacked at once.

They attacked. And colliding one with another, they began to fight among themselves.

Dr. Scarabus' face grew hard with fury.

Dr. Craven sat smiling in his chair, which was floating in the air directly above the snarling gray. After a moment, he leaned forward and waved his hand over the beasts. Instantly, the snarling changed to a faint, pathetic yipping. The four great beasts had become so many puppies, tiny and ludicrous, mewling angrily.

Dr. Scarabus glared at them, gestured, made them disappear. Then he glared up at his still smiling opponent and gestured again.

Dr. Craven's chair began to float downward. And as he rode it toward the floor, Dr. Craven's smile tightened. His eyes remained on Scarabus; his hands didn't move.

But one of Dr. Scarabus' hands had moved, subtly and covertly. And with that movement, a large square of floor was gone from beneath Erasmus Craven's chair.

Not until the chair began to move down through the hole did Dr. Craven realize that something was amiss. Then, glancing into the pit below, he saw the darkly churning waters, and rising from them, the crocodiles, red eyed, jagged toothed, snapping viciously. He gasped in horror; and with a quick gesture, made the chair bob back up and the square of floor return.

Together, the chair and the magician bounced to rest, and now, looking toward his opponent, Erasmus Craven gasped once more.

Sitting in Dr. Scarabus' place was Roderick Craven, his eyes open and staring, a lock of hair noticeably missing from his forehead, one withered finger beginning to flex up and out. Suddenly, that finger was in the air, the hideous black nail pointing straight forward, and a heavy-shafted black lance fly as if from out of it—to penetrate the body opposite.

There was an ugly splintering sound as the lance came through the back of Erasmus Craven's chair, and over that sound there were the sounds of Estelle Craven's screams, Rexford Bedlo's gagging, the dull whine of the raven—and the softly melodious, the diabolical, chuckles that issued from Lenore.

The corpse had disappeared, and Dr. Scarabus was again sitting in the chair opposing that of Erasmus Craven. Smiling without humor, Dr. Scarabus got to his feet and moved across the arena to inspect his victim. He looked first at the lance, which was impaling a chest without motion, a chest without breath. Then, leaning closer, smiling more broadly, and more evilly, he looked into his victim's eyes, eyes that were glazed and staring, and set into a face which was obviously that of a dead man.

Pleased with his victory, he stood straight and was about to turn around when a faint, a barely audible noise, a kind of slow whispering or rustling, made him bend again and look again at the lance. Not blood, but sawdust was running from the wound around it. What he had heard was the sound of that sawdust trickling to the floor.

He straightened abruptly now, realizing that he had been duped into thinking that the sawdust-filled dummy in the chair was Dr. Craven. Again, he was about to turn. But now, suddenly an egg broke across the top of his head; Yoke and white dribbled down his hair, into his eyes.

With a grimace of fury, he wiped at his eyes and looked upward. He had just time enough to see his opponent's legs dangling from the chandelier above. Then the second egg descended, this one smashing itself in the exact center of his forehead. Growling as if demented, he wiped his eyes once more—and in so doing, managed to make a rapid and unexpected gesture in Dr. Craven's direction.

The chandelier plummeted to the floor, carrying a startled looking Erasmus Craven with it, and then, somehow, crashing with that startled looking magician beneath its full weight.

This time, Dr. Scarabus was not so ready to believe the evidence of Estelle's screams and Lenore's chuckles—and what he thought he saw. He looked around suspiciously; he looked up, looked down; he strode the length and the breadth of the entry hall, looking. And he listened keenly, intently. Only after he had taken these precautions did he allow himself the pleasure of a grim smile.

He had beaten Craven at last. Now he approached the body, smiled down at it with evil satisfaction, and reached forward with his right foot, kicked it lightly. It cracked open—releasing a swift flurry of doves into the hall.

Dr. Scarabus staggered back. He gestured, and the doves no longer existed. Then, with a soundless snarl, he whirled about, enraged at having been made the fool twice over. Suddenly, he stiffened, glowered at that spot from which he had heard a low, teasing whistle.

There, in his chair—in Dr. Scarabus' chair—was Erasmus Craven. Erasmus Craven was sitting back, and Erasmus Craven was smiling impassively at him.

Starting to break from this assault on his nerves, Dr. Scarabus gestured furiously. A huge fireball shot out from his two hands and hurtled toward Dr. Craven—who calmly motioned it to the side, where it burst against the wall and spread flame in every direction.

Too furious now to think, Dr. Scarabus propelled one fireball after another at his smiling adversary. And he watched one fireball after another get deflected, each in a different direction, each to burst open in a different place and set fire to a different part of the hall.

For a moment, Dr. Scarabus stood still, his face distorted by frustrations, his features twitching with rage—and with the efforts of thought. Then, abruptly, he gestured upward with both hands. There was a roaring overhead, and a gigantic section of the ceiling fell straight toward Dr. Craven, crashing down over him and temporarily obscuring him from sight in a thick shower of debris, a swirling cloud of mortar dust.

When the dust and the debris had settled, however, Dr. Scarabus was able to see Erasmus Craven, still smiling, still unperturbed. Above Dr. Craven, quivering slightly as it hung suspended in mid-air, was a large protective canopy. Fragments of the ceiling were heaped on top of it; a few were tumbling harmlessly from its edges.

Dr. Scarabus gasped. Still standing near the fallen chandelier, he began, almost maniacally, to gnash his teeth. Then, all of a sudden, he clenched them. Once more, his expression was hard, concentrated.

He started walking toward his opponent.

And smiling no longer, Erasmus Craven rose and walked forward to meet him.

From the balcony, Estelle, Rexford, and the raven watched in bated silence.

On the top step, Lenore stood up, clutched at the banister rail, leaned tensely against it. She, too, was silent.

The contestants had stopped moving. Each knew that this was to be the decisive clash. They looked at each other in harsh, adamantine silence.

At last, very slowly, very deliberately, Dr. Scarabus raised his arms straight ahead of him.

And Dr. Craven did the same thing, but a little more quickly, so that the two magicians came to be pointing at each other in exactly the same instant.

Then, without hesitation, without wavering, without delay, each of the two sent forth from his fingertips a cloud of pure force. Then clouds met, and with a hideous whirring and shrieking, began to grind against each other.

Except for the vibrations of their fingers, the magicians were motionless—opposing statues from which poured incredible energy. Each man was putting every bit of strength he had into this last attempt on the other; each was struggling to summon more. The force fields were mounting in size and in intensity. The floor began to shudder.

Stronger the forces grew, and stronger. The whirring grew louder; the shrieking so shrill as to be almost unbearable. And now the whole castle started to vibrate, its very wall a tremble.

The battle could not go on much longer; one man had to weaken.

And that man was Dr. Scarabus.

Little by little, his cloud of force began to shrivel and contract. As it did, Erasmus Craven's replaced it, crowding in around it, and slowly and inexorably, pushing it back. The noise stopped. The castle quivered slightly and then no more. Dr. Craven moved closer to Scarabus, and closer yet as the old man's resistance was consumed—and finally gone.

Dr. Craven dropped his hands. His cloud, too, was gone. He shook his wrists to rid them of their aching stiffness. Then he looked down at Scarabus—and saw not a great sorcerer, more cunning, more dreadful, and stronger than any other, but a pitiably wrinkled old man, powerless, quaking, on his knees.

"*Kill* him! the raven shouted excitedly. "*Kill* Him! Destroy the old monster!"

Meekly and in silence, Dr. Scarabus waited for his destruction to come.

For a moment or so, Dr. Craven seemed to be considering it. Then, with a sigh, he turned his back to the defeated old man, and sighing again, he moved toward the staircase. Dr. Scarabus' expression was lifeless as he watched him pick his way through the rubble of the contest, and finally, start to ascend.

Lenore had rearranged the fold and billows of her white gown. She had pulled the crimson shawl tighter across her shoulders, draped it a little differently over the fullness of her bosom. She had wet her lips and left them parted slightly in appeal.

Thus prepared, she drifted down the stairs to meet the victorious magician. "Erasmus! *Darling,*" she breathed, opening her great black eyes wide. "The very moment you defeated him, it seemed as if a—*cloud* were lifted from my mind.

He looked at her without emotion, seeing her clearly for perhaps the first time.

And now she threw herself upon him, clung pantingly to him. "I'm free of his control at last! Oh, Erasmus, I'm so happy. Take me away from here, darling. Take me home."

He neither spoke nor moved.

"Erasmus," she said softly, a little worried now and a little confused, and she drew back to gaze at him—and to allow him to gaze upon her beauty, and to succumb to it, as he always had, as every man had, always.

But he was released. It was he who had been set free, not she. He looked at her just once more, and that look was no more than a glance, hard and cold and appraising. Then, brushing past her, he continued up the stairs. Estelle was waiting for him at the top of the flight, slumped against Rexford, so weak with relief that she was unable to come down.

Shocked, Lenore called after her husband, softly at first, "Erasmus! What is it, darling?" Then, getting desperate when he didn't turn, when he seemed not even to have heard, she fairly shouted, "Don't you understand? Dr. Scarabus had me under his control. I didn't know what I was doing! I—"

But Erasmus Craven was already embracing Estelle, smiling down at her, and pressing her against him happily/ "Let us go home, my dear," he said to his daughter. And to Rexford Bedlo, "Come along, young sir."

They—Erasmus Craven, Estelle, Rexford and the raven, which was still sitting on Rexford's shoulder—passed Lenore as they descended to the entry hall. But none of them paid her any notice.

"Erasmus," she cried self-pityingly. "How can you *do* this to me?"

He had his arm around Estelle and was guiding her toward the door.

"Erasmus!"

For an instant, his face tightened as a final pang of anguish for Lenore—his Lenore—threatened to overcome him. But he didn't turn. He didn't look back. "It's all right my dear," he said to Estelle. And as she glanced at him, and he knew that she understood, he repeated firmly, *It's all right now.*"

Still on his knees, Dr. Scarabus was staring at the floor with glazed eyes. He was an old man, a beaten man. He whimpered unintelligibly as Estelle and her father, followed by Rexford and the raven, moved past him on their way out.

They looked at him in silence—until the raven said, "You crushed him beautifully, Erasmus."

"*And,*" Dr. Craven answered gravely "in so doing, I resorted to the very force which I have always despised."

"You had to do it, didn't you?"

"I *had* to do it," he said, almost to himself, as he stood at the door with his daughter. Then, turning, and seeing that Rexford and the raven were just behind, he opened the door. "For how many more centuries will men use that remark to justify brutality?"

No one answered him.

The door to Dr. Scarabus' castle had closed, and Dr. Scarabus and Lenore were now alone in the entry hall.

With a great effort, Dr. Scarabus looked up, saw that the walls were afire, some of them about to crack and fall. He shook his head dumbly, informally. Then, crawling at first, and after that, struggling to his feet and walking as if in torment, he made his way to a chair and slumped down on it, exhausted.

After several moments, he looked up again. And now he saw Lenore. She was standing in front of his chair, staring at him scornfully.

"*So,*" she said in a lewdly melodious tone. "*The Grand Master* has been defeated. And folly of follies, he set the whole thing up himself."

She leaned closer to him, smiled into his face to scoff him. "*look* at you. A tired old man," She paused and ran her eyes over him. Then, as he shut his to avoid the return of her gaze, she said, "Was it for *this* that I left my husband?"

Suddenly she stopped, shook herself. There were bits of plaster on her white dress. The ceiling was rumbling now, quickly, faintly.

Once more, Lenore smiled, this time to herself. "And now your castle is falling down. Poor old Dr. Scarabus. He shan't have anything left to call his own." Putting her hands on the arms of his chair, she leaned so close to him now that he was compelled to open his eyes. She waited to add cruelly, "Least of all—*me.*"

Straightening, Lenore had started to turn away—when Dr. Scarabus snaked out his right hand and clamped it over her wrist. She looked at him in shock. Then she tried to pull loose. But his grip was too strong. "*Let go of me,*" she said coldly.

Instead, he drew her down, farther and farther, until he could hiss into her ear. "Not just yet, my dear." Overhead, there was a great rending noise. He listened. And now he smiled. "This particular doom—we shall enjoy together."

Lenore looked up in horror. There were huge rifts in the ceiling, particularly about the edges of the hole that had been made during the contest. Again, Lenore tried to pull herself from Dr. Scarabus' grip. Again, she failed.

And now the rending noise was repeated—louder, sharper. The rifts widened, grew longer, covered all that was left of the ceiling. An enormous fissure opened directly above.

As Lenore was about to scream, there was a deep, thunderous roar, a hideous grumble that seemed to come more from below than elsewhere, and immediately after, the ceiling collapsed, burying Lenore and Dr. Scarabus beneath its weighty fall.

The Cravens' coach had stopped at the sound of distant rumbling. Dr. Craven and Estelle had looked back through the windows; Rexford had turned about on the driver's seat; and the raven had flown from Rexford's shoulder to the roof of the coach. All four had seen Dr. Scarabus' castle crash down to fiery ruin. Then the coach had moved on.

Now Erasmus Craven was looking across his study toward the fire that was blazing on the hearth. Estelle and Rexford Bedlo were sitting on the floor before it, chatting intimately. Dr. Craven smiled.

"*Era*smus." He heard the raven call from behind him, and turning, he moved to the desk, on top of which it was perched.

"Now that Scarabus is out of the way," it said, without so much as giving him a chance to sit down, "we've got to make immediate plans for your assumption of the grand mastership. I'll be glad to act as your liaison so you won't be bothered having to present you case, personally, to the Brotherhood. Later on, I'll be happy to assume the post of—"

"Dr. Bedlo," Erasmus Craven cut in.

"*Yes?*" the bird said brightly.

"Do you really believe that your treachery can be so easily forgiven—and forgotten?"

"Treachery?" the bird asked, offended. "I saved all your lives!"

"Having put them into jeopardy in the first place."

"That's beside the point," the bird said stiffly. It paced about on top of the desk for a few moments; then, stopping, it puffed out its black chest and said, "Very well. If that's the way you feel about it. Kindly return me to my rightful form and I'll leave."

Frowning, Dr. Craven said nothing.

Well?" the bird reminded him sharply.

"I'll take it under advisement, doctor."

"Take it under—! The bird seemed stunned.

"Up." Dr. Craven said, pointing.

"What?"

"Up." Dr. Craven was still pointing. He glared threateningly at the bird.

"Now, wait a minute, Erasmus." It backed off, toward the far edge of the desk.

"Up!" Dr. Craven repeated, pointing still, and glowering ominously.

Whereupon the raven spread its wings and flew toward the hallway door, lighting once more on the bust of Pallas that looked down from above it.

"Well," the bird said, muttering sourly. ""I've never heard of such ingratitude in my entire life. It's getting so you can't trust anybody any more." Then, ruffling its feathers, it settled itself on top of Pallas' marble shoulder, from there to stare down at the study with brooding eyes. "I'm too sweet and gentle, that's my trouble," it said.

"NEVERMORE"

Peter Lorre telling a joke to AIP President James H. Nicholson, Vincent Price and AIP Vice-President Samuel Z. Arkoff (on the left). Film historian William K. Everson visited Peter Lorre on the set of The Raven and when Everson's 3-year old daughter, Bambi saw John Dierkes made-up as the decaying corpse of Roderick Craven, she asked Lorre if Dierkes "was a good monster or a bad monster?" Lorre looked around before he whispered to her in his famous voice, "Oh, it's a bad monster. There are no good monsters at American International."

The Making of The Raven

By
Lawrence French

Interviews with
Vincent Price
Roger Corman
Richard Matheson

"The screens three Titians of Terror united for the first time on screen." Boris Karloff, Peter Lorre and Vincent Price spent half a day in the studio posing for publicity shots taken by photographer Bill Creamer to promote The Raven.

"In a publicity story for The Raven, AIP noted that star "Vincent Price has been terrified of snakes all his life, and as seen in this photo, he had to face up to his fear for a scene which required that he have a huge snake entwined about his neck. To his great surprise, despite apprehension beforehand, his fear disappeared easily when he saw the snake trainer fondle the reptile before the shot."

VINCENT PRICE
ON
THE RAVEN

Interviewed By

LAWRENCE FRENCH

LAWRENCE FRENCH: You must have enjoyed making The Raven with Boris Karloff and Peter Lorre.

VINCENT PRICE: Oh Yes, we had a wonderful time. They were both divine people, with great senses of humor. We used to sit around and say very seriously, "How can we scare the little bastards!" We'd say, "Let's do this, let's do that, let's do the other thing." One time, one of the big magazines, *Look* or *Life*, had sent out a reporter to try and make fun of us. He came on the set and was really sort of grand you know, and when he saw that we were really enjoying making the picture, he wrote the most wonderful article about the joy we had in making something that was really pure entertainment.

LAWRENCE FRENCH: You've often remarked how on The Raven it was the actors idea to make fun of the story.

VINCENT PRICE: Well, what happened was that when Boris, Peter and I heard we were all going to be in *The Raven* together, we were really very excited. We called each other up, and Boris said to me, "Have you read the poem lately?" I said, "Yes" and Boris said "What's the plot?"

Of course there is no plot. Then, after we read the script we thought it was great fun, particularly the magic thing that went on between the three of us, but basically the script had nothing at all to do with Poe's poem. So what we did was try to figure out among ourselves what we could do to send it up. It was really more of the actors in that instance, than it was Roger. I did a thing in the very first scene where I'm walking across my

129

study. You know, I hear the knocking at the window, and I hit my head on the telescope and when I walk back, I hit my head on the telescope again, so immediately the audience knew that something was a little bit wrong.

LAWRENCE FRENCH: Then, right after that you solemnly say to Peter Lorre, "Shall I ever see the rare and radiant Lenore again?"

VINCENT PRICE: And Peter came up with that marvelous line, "How the hell should I know!" That was an absolutely gorgeous line.

LAWRENCE FRENCH: Later, when you go down to the crypt, Peter Lorre looks around at all the dust and dirt and says nonchalantly, "Hard place to keep clean?"

VINCENT PRICE: Yes, that was all Peter. Peter had a genius for not saying many of the lines in the script, but he knew them all. He felt, and rightly so I suppose, being as famous a character as he was, that what the audience wanted to see was Peter Lorre, and in a way he was right. I think he started out as an actor, but ended up becoming a fellow named Peter Lorre.

There was one scene in *The Raven* where we had a great deal of exposition, which you always do in those kinds of things. How we get from one place to another, and Peter was sort of vamping until ready, carrying on and so-forth, so I finally said to him, "Come on Peter, for God's sake just say the lines!" Peter looked at me and said, "Do you really mean that old boy" and I said, "Yes!" so he said every line that was in the script. He just got on with it, but he loved to invent. I think that it was part of his training in Germany, that there was a lot of improvisation going on in pictures like *M* (Peter Lorre's first film, done for Fritz Lang in 1931).

LAWRENCE FRENCH: Roger Corman said that you would go along with Peter Lorre's improvisations, but Boris Karloff was unable to go along with them.

VINCENT PRICE: You know, I'm an actor who knows every line in the script, because I don't know how else to do it. I am not geared to improvise. But if you're working with someone who is improvising, you improvise too. There's no other way to do it. You have to go along with their gags.

LAWRENCE FRENCH: So you went along with Peter's gags and Boris Karloff would get somewhat upset with them?

VINCENT PRICE: I don't think Boris was ever upset with it, not really. I think Boris didn't have as much to do with Peter as I did, in the story.

LAWRENCE FRENCH: Yes, it was more of you and Peter Lorre versus Boris Karloff and Hazel Court.

VINCENT PRICE: That's right, and my whole thing was with Peter. An awful lot of those lines like, "Hard place to keep clean," and all of that was really Peter. He was a very funny man—a very funny man. One time we were sitting around talking, and I said to Peter "It always kills me that in these pictures I keep my family conveniently buried downstairs in the crypt. Well Peter thought that was hysterical, so that's where another one of his ad-lib's came from. When I said "My father's interred below," Peter said "Where else?"

LAWRENCE FRENCH: I loved the magic duel at the end of the picture. You and Boris Karloff start off deadly serious, but it soon degenerates into a complete farce. Did you or Boris Karloff have any difficulties doing those scenes?

VINCENT PRICE: Well, Boris hated being strung up in the air on those chairs. He was terribly crippled and we were both floating in the air on these wires. It wasn't a pleasant feeling! And I hated having that snake wrapped around my neck for two hours. Boris throws a scarf at me and it's supposed to turn into a snake, and I hate snakes. I asked Roger how he was going to handle the scene and he said he had a man who was a snake trainer who was going to come in. The snake trainer told me not to worry, because it was a very tame boa constrictor and boa's don't actually bite. Well, the scene began with the snake around my neck, but Roger wanted it with its head facing the camera and it wouldn't turn that way, so we had to fuss with it for over an hour to finally get the shot and then the snake started to strangle me because it felt the fur on my costume! With a bit of coaxing we were finally able to get the damn thing off of me.

LAWRENCE FRENCH: Roger said it was a very enjoyable set, except for a couple of tense moments he had with Boris Karloff.

VINCENT PRICE: Well, Roger was very serious, so if you pushed him too far, he felt that he had hired you and you should just get on with it. But we were all people who knew our jobs. We didn't waste any time saying, "I can't play this scene because I don't feel it." You felt it, or else you didn't play it!

LAWRENCE FRENCH: I imagine you didn't have time for much rehearsal on such short shooting schedules.

VINCENT PRICE: No we didn't, and as you know, in movies there is very seldom any rehearsal time at all. But Roger had a marvelous way of cheating. Of course, all actors like to rehearse, so Roger would get Boris and Peter and myself and whoever was to be in the picture to come down and read, and we'd have a sort of great discussion. I think we would do one day of that and then we were supposed to be paid.

We all really welcomed the chance to be able to walk around on the sets and sort of familiarize ourselves with what the ambiance of the story was. It was not so much of a characterization rehearsal, as a run-through. We'd just walk around the sets and Roger would say, "This is what will happen here." Then we'd move onto the next set. And we all went along with it, because it meant so much to us. We all got so carried away, knowing that the schedule was so short. We'd end up doing about two days of that before shooting began. I always thought Roger was very smart in doing that.

LAWRENCE FRENCH: Of course, Roger also had everything carefully pre-planned, didn't he?

VINCENT PRICE: Very much so. Very much. It was really a lot of fun. Roger also had a genius for surrounding himself with the best people he could find. Floyd Crosby, Danny Haller and everyone we worked with, they were all among the best in the business. It was like a little stock company. You knew the technicians and the other actors, so you could work better with them. It was like what Ingmar Bergman had done so brilliantly in Sweden.

LAWRENCE FRENCH: It's too bad you couldn't have done a few more pictures with Boris Karloff.

VINCENT PRICE: Yes, Boris has been gone for some twenty years now, and I've been around and almost gone for nearly as long. I've always given him credit for an awful lot. He was really the first one, and he had a great pride in doing these pictures. I felt an enormous closeness as a friend and a co-worker in Boris, and this marvelous sort of warmth as a human being. We used to go out to dinner in London, which was wonderful fun, because the two of us would walk into a restaurant and we would clear the place. We never had to make reservations, because we had our choice of any table!

LAWRENCE FRENCH: Peter Lorre died the year after you made The Raven and you delivered the eulogy at his funeral.

VINCENT PRICE: Yes, Peter and I had the same agent (Lester Salkow), so one day I got a call from my agent and he said, "Peter is dead." It was extraordinary because his wife was that very day going down to get a divorce and she found him dead. So instead of being his ex-wife, she became his widow. So my agent said, "It's terrible; all of Peter's friends are dead. Who are we going to get to read the eulogy?" You know, the fat man, Sydney Greenstreet, he had died, and so had Bogart. So I said "I've known Peter a long time, I'd be delighted to do it." Then the day of his funeral I was doing a Red Skelton show. I wrote the eulogy and I went to Red and said, "Red, you know Peter died yesterday morning, would you mind if I took an extra hour off for lunch, because I'm going to his funeral and read the eulogy." So Red said, "Peter's dead? We'll all go!" So the entire company went to Peter's funeral, which was marvelous.

Peter Lorre as Dr. Bedloe attempts to prove his mastery of magic by challenging Dr. Scarabus to a duel.

Richard Matheson named Lorre's magician after the character of Augustus Bedloe in Poe's story of reincarnation, A Tale of the Ragged Mountains.

PETER LORRE

June 26, 1904 – March 23, 1964

Excerpts from Vincent Price's Eulogy:

Peter had no illusions about our profession. He loved to entertain, to be a face maker, as he said often of our kind. But his was a face that registered the thoughts of an inquisitive mind and his receptive heart, and the audience, which was his world, loved him for the glimpses he gave them of that heart and mind.

Peter held back nothing of himself. He always seemed to be exploring you. The aura of devotion that surrounded him made all men glad to be his friend, to feed him and be fed in turn.

That something sad about him and a certain necessary madness went together to capture the hearts and give his fellow players pause, lest they be unprepared to match his winsomeness. This was a man to be aware of at all times, for he was well aware of all who shared the stage with him, and working with him never failed to fulfill the seventh and perhaps most sacred sense—the sense of fun.

Roger Corman directing Peter Lorre and William Baskin for the ax-duel sequence in The Raven. *Roger Corman laughingly recalled that Peter Lorre told him to make sure Bill Baskin missed him while he was welding the ax as Grimes, the possessed servant of Dr. Craven.*

ROGER CORMAN
ON
THE RAVEN

Interviewed By

LAWRENCE FRENCH

LAWRENCE FRENCH: When you decided to make The Raven, *you obviously couldn't remain faithful to the source material, because it's only an eighteen-stanza poem. Vincent Price said he got together with Boris Karloff and Peter Lorre to dream up some of the broader situations in the script and make it a comedy, since there basically was no story to the poem.*

ROGER CORMAN: (Astonished) That is totally false! I don't know what Vincent was thinking of. Dick Matheson and I worked out that script in great detail and it had been conceived of as a comedy from the very beginning. I felt that we had been successful with *The Black Cat* episode in *Tales of Terror* of bringing humor into the story, so we decided to vary the approach once again for *The Raven*. So it became a comedy within the horror background. Now I can say this: We did more improvisation on that film then any of the others. However, the picture followed exactly the line of the script. We only improvised dialogue within scenes. One of the reasons for that was because Peter Lorre was a great improvisational actor, who did not always learn his lines, but would come up with great ideas.

It was very interesting working with those three actors, because I liked some of the things Peter was doing, and Vincent could play along and do a little bit of it too. Boris Karloff, however, came in totally prepared and was really unable to improvise. So Boris would come in and find that Peter would often be making up dialogue that was really very funny. So early on in the shooting, the second day I think, Boris came to me and said, "Roger, look I'm taking this part seriously, I know all my lines, but Peter never gives me my cue line." I said, "Boris, I'll talk to Peter about it but you have to understand that Peter was trained in Germany with Bertold Brecht and you have to try and be a little bit looser. So I talked to Peter and told him, "Look, what you're doing is great, but try to stay a bit closer to the script, so you at least start out and end up on the right lines." Boris was a good guy, but he was just a little bit stiff and he really couldn't go along with Peter's improvisations. So it was a little bit touchy working on the set, because Boris was always somewhat annoyed when these changes took place. Vincent was also totally prepared, but he was also able to improvise with the changes Peter was making. But overall, the picture followed exactly the line of the script. The improvisation had to do mostly with a little bit of dialogue changes and some business changes—things that Peter did physically. (Laughs) I think Vincent may have forgotten some of what took place!

LAWRENCE FRENCH: Actually, I may have misstated what Vincent Price said. Apparently he had talked to Peter Lorre and Boris Karloff on the telephone before they even read the script. They all wondered how you and Richard Matheson were going to turn a poem into a movie—which they all agreed was a somewhat ludicrous idea—so they decided the best idea would be to sent it up.

ROGER CORMAN: That may be. I don't say I'm the only one who remembers, but I do remember that there was a script and that it was followed in it's broad outline exactly, scene for scene. The only changes made were some dialogue changes and a great deal of business changes.

LAWRENCE FRENCH: It must have been marvelous working with such a talented cast on The Raven.

ROGER CORMAN: Oh, absolutely! It was a real pleasure. All three of them were superb actors. With some actors you have to keep working on them, imploring them to give a performance, but with Vincent, Peter and Boris as well, they would give you all you could ask for and more. It was really very fascinating to be working with them.

LAWRENCE FRENCH: You also had Jack Nicholson acting in the film, who at the time was quite a young novice.

ROGER CORMAN: Yes, I had used Jack in a number of my earlier films, and as the script for *The Raven* was being developed, it became clear that the character of Peter Lorre's son would be an ideal role for Jack Nicholson to play. I had first met Jack at an acting class taught by Jeff Corey, and we both learned from Jeff how to use little bits of business to create a subtext within a scene. We never had a lot of time for rehearsal, but while Peter was talking to Jack he said, "What if you as my son, want nothing more in the world than my approval, and I as your father, really can't stand you." Well, both Jack and I immediately said, "That's perfect." None of that was in the script, but that made Peter and Jack's scenes together really funny. Jack was always trying to get Peter's approval and Peter would always be pushing him away. So during the scenes between them, Jack would always be fussing and worrying about his father, putting his cloak around him and so-forth, which would annoy Peter to no-end. He'd slap Jack and push him away from him whenever he started to do that. That was really a lot of fun.

Peter also came up with some great lines for *The Raven*. In one scene he had this feathered costume on Vincent said to Peter, "My Father is interred below." We rehearsed the scene and Peter didn't say anything, but just read it as it was scripted, but when we shot it, Peter added the line, "Where else?" Vincent went right along with it and I said, "Print it, we're going with that." Then when they go down to the crypt, they open up the coffin and Peter is standing there and they look down at the decayed body of Vincent's father and the coffin lid drops and Peter let one of his feathered arms get caught in it and yelled out, "Oh, my arm." In another scene, Peter had to run away from William Baskin, after he becomes possessed and starts to attack Peter with an ax. When I rehearsed the scene, William Baskin was swinging the ax at Peter like he was really out of control, so Peter got a little bit worried about it. Right before we shot it, Peter said to me, "Roger, just one thing: make sure that guy misses me!"

LAWRENCE FRENCH: Vincent Price said he really enjoyed the shooting of The Raven and I imagine you probably tried to maintain a jovial atmosphere on the set.

ROGER CORMAN: Yes, particularly since we were playing *The Raven* for humor. I haven't done that much comedy, but when I have, I've tried to keep that feeling going both on and off the set. You can't very well be working intensely serious in the preparation, and then come in and tell somebody to be funny for three minutes in front of the camera, and then go back. I think you have to try and maintain that spirit all day long, as much as possible. And because it was a comedy, I took a different approach not only towards the acting, but also with the sets and the photography. It was not nearly as somber as I had used in the earlier films. Overall, I would say that we had as good a spirit on the set of *The Raven* as any film I've ever worked on, except for a couple of moments with Boris. There was a slight edge to it, because Boris came in with a carefully worked out preparation, so when Peter started improvising new lines it really threw Boris off from his preparation.

LAWRENCE FRENCH: At the time Boris Karloff was 75 years old and wasn't in the best of health. Richard Matheson said he was watching the scene where Boris had to walk down a flight of steps and it was very difficult for him.

ROGER CORMAN: That's right. Danny Haller had designed this beautiful long staircase and Boris was supposed to appear at the top of the staircase and walk down it to meet Vincent and Peter at the bottom. Boris was very frail so he came to me and said, "Roger, I can't walk down that staircase." I said, "All right, here's what we'll do. I'll have two guys off camera to help you and just take two steps and then I'll cut away to a reaction shot of Jack Nicholson. Then we'll bring you down to the bottom of the stairs, and we'll do the same thing, you'll just take two steps at the bottom of the staircase and we'll continue the scene with Vincent and Peter."

LAWRENCE FRENCH: Boris Karloff was quoted in an interview for Films and Filming (May, 1965) by Robin Bean, saying that if he asked you for advice on how to play a scene you'd say, "You're experienced actors, get on with it! I've got the camera, my lighting and the angles. I know how I'm going to put this together."

ROGER CORMAN: (Surprised) That is completely and totally false! I would have never said something like that. It's ridiculous. I would work with Boris and discuss the role as with any actor. I doubt that Boris said that. I would think it's a misquote. I have been misquoted so many times myself, I'm sure Boris was misquoted. In the first place, such a thing would never have happened, and secondly, Boris would never say something like that.

LAWRENCE FRENCH: Perhaps Karloff had the impression you were more concerned with the camera set-ups, and not enough with the actors performances.

ROGER CORMAN: He might have had some such impression, but I always tried to work as much as I possibly could with the actors on a short shooting schedule. It's quite clear that if you're shooting a picture in 15 days, you're not going to have as much time working with the actors, as if you had 100 days. On a longer schedule you'd be able to get more rehearsal time, but unfortunately that is one of the drawbacks of low-budget productions. Usually what I'd do is talk with the actors before the picture was even shot. I would bring the whole cast in before shooting, and we'd discuss the characters, relationships and so forth, because during shooting there would be time for only a small amount of rehearsal. In fact, sometimes what I would do is, while the crew was lighting the next set-up, I would step away from the set and go over what we would be doing in the next scene. That way we could rehearse and have a run-through if the set we were going to use wasn't ready for us.

LAWRENCE FRENCH: It may be that Karloff was thinking more about *The Terror, which he said you wanted to shoot in only two days in order to* *utilize the sets left over from The Raven.*

ROGER CORMAN: That's right. What happened was that at the end of shooting on *The Raven* I talked to Boris to see if he would agree to work for two days on another picture. Boris looked at the script—except at that point all I had was an outline and a few of Boris's scenes written—and I said, "Boris, this is going to be a tough one. We're going to have to shoot it in only two days," and he agreed to make it. I think it must have been in the back of his mind that I wasn't really going to do it in two days. You know how people sometimes say they're going to do something, but they never really do it. Well, we had to do it in two days, because that was all the money I had. So Boris knew what he was getting into, although I don't think he realized it meant he'd be working steadily from the time he got on the set in the morning, until the end of the day. Actors don't normally work that way, which is why Boris was somewhat upset.

What actually happened was that Danny Haller had done such great sets for *The Raven*, before the last week of shooting I said to Dan, "It's really a shame we have to tear these sets down." I had a little bit of money, but only enough for two days of shooting, so I decided to try and come up with a story outline for another horror picture we could make in two days. So I called up Leo Gordon, a friend of mine who had written *The Wasp*

Woman and asked him if he could write scenes for a picture using the castle sets Dan had done for *The Raven*. *The Terror* ended up having the longest list of un-credited directors of any film I ever made. I started shooting it on the sets we had used for *The Raven*, then Francis Coppola took over. Francis got another job and then Monte Hellman took over. When Monte Hellman left, Jack Hill took over.

LAWRENCE FRENCH: Considering it's cost, The Raven is really quite an impressive picture. Especially with all the special effects required for the magic duel between Vincent Price and Boris Karloff.

ROGER CORMAN: Yes, I felt *The Raven* had the biggest look of any of the Poe films I made in America. Danny Haller was able to create lavish sets using units from the previous pictures, so we got a great look without spending a lot of money. The picture ended up costing around $350,000. Within the limitations of that budget, I felt the duel between Vincent and Boris came off very well. It was all planned out very carefully in advance and we were able to achieve some interesting optical effects when they were hurling the thunderbolts at each other.

LAWRENCE FRENCH: Vincent Price told me he was not too crazy about being suspended in mid-air when he had to levitate on his chair during the duel scene.

ROGER CORMAN: That's right and we had a very difficult time getting those shots. What we ended up doing was putting Vincent in his chair, and then put the chair on the end of a camera crane and then I shot him from below, so you would see him in the air, but you don't see that he's actually seated on the crane arm. Then we simply moved the crane all over the set, so it looked liked he was flying through the air. Today of course, that could all be done digitally.

LAWRENCE FRENCH: It seems rather incredible that you could get such intricate tracking and dolly shots on only a three week shooting schedule. How many takes would you generally shoot before you were satisfied?

ROGER CORMAN: I averaged about three. I would very seldom print the first take. I would sometimes print the first, but I would generally print take two, three or four. I would say I averaged about three or four takes.

LAWRENCE FRENCH: There was an 1982 article in Film Comment by David Chute, "The New World of Roger Corman," that quoted Vincent Price as swearing, "So long as the camera didn't tip over, Corman almost always printed the first take." I imagine that's another misquote, because Vincent Price told me exactly the opposite, namely "That you worked all day on setting up your shots."

ROGER CORMAN: (Laughing) Yes, I'm sure that's not an accurate quote. Not only is that not true, but I would say I almost never printed the first take, for a number of reasons. Primarily, there was the possibility of something going wrong to the film in the lab, so I would generally want two complete takes, just for protection. Then if something went wrong in the lab, I would have the unprinted take to fall back on. So for that reason, I would say that I printed fewer first takes then anybody, even through I was working very rapidly.

LAWRENCE FRENCH: It's probably a story that would be more accurate about one of your earlier films, like The Little Shoppe Of Horrors, which you shot in only three days.

ROGER CORMAN: Yes, stories build upon each other and I know that not everything that has been published about me is totally accurate. There's a tendency of people to remember things differently, particularly if they happened a number of years ago. It gets filtered through their memory or their own persona and they sometimes elaborate just for the sake of telling a good story. So the story builds and takes on a different direction.

LAWRENCE FRENCH: On The Shining, Jack Nicholson was doing 60 or 70 takes before Stanley Kubrick was satisfied.

ROGER CORMAN: Jack made a great comment about that. Kubrick had gone to over 100 takes on one shot, and after it was all over Jack said to him, "You know Stanley this is all very well and good, but I generally peak around the 50th take."

RICHARD MATHESON
ON
THE RAVEN

Interviewed By

LAWRENCE FRENCH

LAWRENCE FRENCH: After doing The Black Cat episode of Tales of Terror as a horror-comedy, you turned your script for your next Poe film, The Raven into a complete comedy.

RICHARD MATHESON: Well, after I heard they wanted to make a movie out of a poem, I felt that was an utter joke, so comedy was really the only way to go with it.

LAWRENCE FRENCH: Vincent Price said Peter Lorre did a lot of on-set improvisations while shooting The Raven.

RICHARD MATHESON: They improvised comedy bits. I'm sure Peter Lorre would improvise the whole movie if he could. I think Peter knew generally what the story was, but whether he knew the lines and his memory didn't function that well, or whether he just didn't bother to learn more than the general substance of the script, I don't know. He was such a charming man though you couldn't get angry with him. Ordinarily I would have hated that. Everyone else though—Karloff, Rathbone, Price—they all read my lines, word for word, from the script.

LAWRENCE FRENCH: Roger Corman said Peter Lorre's improvisations would really upset Boris Karloff.

RICHARD MATHESON: I'm sure any professional actor would be upset. I'm sure Rathbone was upset too, because it throws them off their own pitch. They're prepared and then get things thrown at them that they're not prepared for, so it makes them look bad. It really isn't professional, nor is it fair. It's just that Peter had always been that way. When he was

144

at Warner Bros. he used to do that with Sidney Greenstreet. He told me how he used to drive Sidney Greenstreet right out of his mind, because he was a letter-perfect actor and Lorre would just throw lines at him that weren't in the script and Greenstreet wouldn't know what in God's name was happening!

LAWRENCE FRENCH: Other than the improvisations that occurred by the actors, did Roger Corman or AIP ever ask you to make any substantial changes to your scripts?

RICHARD MATHESON: No. That was the good thing about those films. They never changed the wordage of my scripts. Sometimes they would tell me to cut something, because they thought it was too long. Then, when they went to shoot it, they'd find it was too short, so I had to add something back while they were shooting. My scripts seemed to read longer then they played. They always did that, but I don't know why.

LAWRENCE FRENCH: Did you visit the set of any of the Poe films while they were shooting them?

RICHARD MATHESON: Yes, I was on the set of *The Raven*, but not very often. It's the most boring thing in the world standing around on a film set. And when I was on the set, it was strictly as a spectator. I never made any script changes on the set. The one thing I remember Roger saying the most is, "We're on the wrong set." As soon as he finished a shot he'd run over to the next set and start setting up a new shot. That's how he made those pictures in only three weeks.

LAWRENCE FRENCH: Of the Poe films, which do you think turned out the best?

RICHARD MATHESON: Probably, I liked *The Raven* the best, but if you say Poe, I suppose the first picture *The House Of Usher* was the purest. The last segment of *Tales Of Terror, The Facts in the Case of M. Valdemar* was pretty well done. It was pretty straight, except I added the doctor and Valemar's wife to the story.

LAWRENCE FRENCH: Roger said he didn't like the Valdemar script because it wasn't cinematic enough—he felt it was too much like a stage play, because it all takes place in only two rooms.

RICHARD MATHESON: That's the reason I liked it. They acted it pretty well, for a change. Vincent and Basil Rathbone were excellent in it, as were Debra Paget and David Frankham. Rathbone was a consummate professional, and I remember talking with him one day and he told me about doing the duel scene with Errol Flynn in *Robin Hood*. He said they'd take three days to shoot a duel scene like that at Warner Bros., while at AIP Roger would shoot the whole *Valdemar* episode in only a week!

LAWRENCE FRENCH: After The Raven, you wrote The Comedy of Terrors but I understand it wasn't as successful as the Poe films at the box-office.

RICHARD MATHESON: It actually made its money back. It didn't lose any money. They told me that the title itself cost them a lot. It's such a contradiction in terms, though. Terror sells and comedy makes them go away, so it's like they're walking in two directions at once. But I thought it was very clever to do a take off on Shakespeare's *The Comedy of Errors*.

LAWRENCE FRENCH: Given it's all star cast of horror actors and the situations you came up with, I'm surprised AIP didn't call it Edgar Allan Poe's Comedy Of Terrors.

RICHARD MATHESON: I think they were probably sorry they didn't use a Poe title, because Poe had a certain marketability. I guess they couldn't quite figure out how to market it. But that was the last one, because I was getting tired of writing about people being buried alive, so I decided to made a joke about it.

LAWRENCE FRENCH: The Raven was actually your last Poe picture. After that Corman hired your friend Charles Beaumont to write The Haunted Palace and The Masque of the Red Death. What did you think of the later Poe films?

RICHARD MATHESON: I thought they were very well done. But I never liked Poe's stories, per se. I can look at them and see how well they're done, but the subject matter itself never really excited me, so I can't really say "I like them."

BORIS KARLOFF
on
THE RAVEN

You first worked with director Roger Corman on *The Raven*, co-starring with Vincent Price and Peter Lorre. I imagine you enjoyed making that picture.

BORIS KARLOFF: Yes, I actually enjoy most of my films, and this one was no exception. We had Peter Lorre looking frightfully funny, like a chubby little black bird. He delighted the whole crew. I've now worked with Roger Corman twice, on *The Raven* and *The Terror*. You see Corman's strong point is as a technician—with the camera and so on. He expects the actors to get on with it, and I know Vincent, Peter and I had to find our own way around, because he had all he wanted. He said, "You're experienced actors, get on with it. I've got the camera, my lighting, the angles and I know how I'm going to put this together." If you asked him about advice on a scene, he'd say, "That's your pigeon... go on, I'm busy with this." This is true for the average film made under these circumstances. The director has his hands full with the mechanics of making the film, and the actor is supposed to know his job well enough to be able to give the director what he wants.

In *The Raven*, my character had to wear this long velvet cape, an immense garment that seemed to weigh a ton. After dragging the bloody thing around behind me for a day or two on the set, I approached Roger and suggested, in my most gracious fashion that the character I played would look much more sinister and effective without the cape. But Roger caught on. He knew why I wanted to get rid of the thing. He just looked at me and said, "Wear the cape Boris." So that was that. Right after *The Raven* I did *The Terror*. It was a real quickie, done in two days. Corman had the sketchiest outline of a story. I read it and begged him not to do it. He said, "That's all right, Boris, I know just what I'm going to do. I want you for two days on this." I was in every shot, of course. Sometimes I was just walking through and then I would change my jacket and walk back. He nearly killed me on the last day. He had me in a tank of cold water for about two hours. After he got me in the can, he suspended operations and went off and directed two or three films to get the money, I suppose, to complete this one. Then off he went and shot the rest of the story somewhere on location in northern California. What he really wanted to do was to shoot the sets of *The Raven,* which were still standing, and were so magnificent. They were done by Daniel Haller and as they were being pulled down around our ears, Roger was dashing around with me and a camera, two steps ahead of the wreckers. It was very funny.

The Raven was made by American International Pictures. How do you like working for them?

BORIS KARLOFF: Oh, they (James Nicholson and Samuel Arkoff, the heads of AIP) have been extremely considerate to me. They are very successful and intelligent men. They know their market and they know their field very well. I'm most grateful to them. Their films are beautifully mounted and photographed. They shoot them in about three weeks. How can they do them in that short amount of time? The answer is in the immense amount of preparation, the homework that is done before you ever get on the set and start shooting. That's when all the money starts to roll out, the moment you assemble the whole thing on the set. Then, if you're not ready, you're throwing money out the window. They rent space at a studio, they have assembled one of the finest crews that I've ever known, and the crews in the studios out there are really marvelous. They anticipate everything, they are ahead of you, they take a pride in what they are doing, and believe me it makes a difference. Everything is there and ready right down to the last button so that there is no pressure on me as an actor. If I've played a scene badly and want to do it again, they say, "Sure," not, "Oh, Christ we haven't got the time."

Boris Karloff comments taken from an interview with William F. Nolan that appeared in *Famous Monsters of Filmland* #30 and Robin Bean in *Films and Filming* magazine (May, 1965).

6214-P17

In 1963 Boris Karloff returned to the screen after a four year absence to play the sinister magician Dr. Scarabus in The Raven. Roger Corman and Boris Karloff went on to make two more movies together: The Terror, and what Mr. Karloff always considered his favorite "final" picture, Peter Bogdanovich's Targets in 1968. The young Jack Nicholson enjoyed working with Karloff immensely and learned from the master his own special technique for marking his script to denote his lines, which Nicholson pointed out during the making of another horror movie, Stanley Kubrick's The Shining.

Jack Nicholson as Rexford Bedlo

Jack Nicholson as Rexford Bedloe, greeting Olive Sturgess as Estelle Craven, as Peter Lorre as Dr. Bedloe and Vincent Price as Dr. Craven look on.

Jack Nicholson recalled having a blast shooting the film with Lorre, Karloff and Price, saying "I loved those guys. I sat around with Peter all the time. I was mad about him. They were wonderful. Since it was a comedy, Roger gave us a little more time to improvise on the set. One thing I also remember about The Raven was the bird we used shit endlessly over everybody and everything. It just shit endlessly. My whole right shoulder was constantly covered with raven shit!"

THE RAVEN
(American International Pictures)

Produced and Directed by Roger Corman. Executive Producers: James H. Nicholson and Samuel Z. Arkoff. Screenplay by Richard Matheson, inspired by Edgar Allan Poe's poem, *The Raven*. Music by Les Baxter. Director of Photography: Floyd Crosby, A.S.C. (in Panavision & Pathecolor). Production Designer: Daniel Haller. Film Editor: Ronald Sinclair. Costumes by Marjorie Corso. Production Sound: John Bury. Sound Editor: Gene Corso. Photographic Effects: Larry Butler and Don Glouner. Unit Manager: Robert Agnew. Make-up: Ted Coodley. Assistant Director: Jack Bohrer. Special Effects: Pat Dinga. Music Editor: Eve Newman. Properties: Karl Brainard. Set Decorator: Harry Reif. Hairdresser: Betty Pedretti. Construction Supervisor: Ross Hahn. Production Assistant: Jack Cash. Titles: National Screen Service. Raven Trainer: Moe Disesso. Still Photographer: Bill Creamer. An Alta Vista Production. Filmed at Producers Studio (in three weeks), beginning on September 21, 1962. Released in New York: January 25, 1963. Released in Los Angeles: February, 1963. 86 minutes.

CAST

Dr. Erasmus Craven	VINCENT PRICE
Dr. Adolphus Bedlo	PETER LORRE
Dr. Scarabus	BORIS KARLOFF
Lenore Craven	HAZEL COURT
Rexford Bedlo	JACK NICHOLSON
Estelle Craven	OLIVE STURGESS
Grimes	WILLIAM BASKIN
Gort	AARON SAXON
Maidservant	CONNIE WALLACE
Roderick Craven	JOHN DIERKES

THE RAVEN

Written
by
Richard Matheson